the
celtic
heart

the CELTIC heart

An anthology of prayers and poems
in the Celtic tradition

PAT ROBSON

Fount
An Imprint of HarperCollins*Publishers*

Fount is an Imprint of
HarperCollins*Religious*
Part of HarperCollins*Publishers*
77–85 Fulham Palace Road, London W6 8JB

First published in Great Britain in 1998
by HarperCollins*Religious*
1 3 5 7 9 10 8 6 4 2

A catalogue record for this book is available
from the British Library.

ISBN 000 628110 9

Printed and bound in Great Britain by Woolnough Bookbinding Ltd,
Irthlingborough, Northamptonshire

To the Companions of St Guenole
and in memory of Bishop Peter Mumford

CONTENTS

SOURCES AND ACKNOWLEDGEMENTS

David Adam is the vicar of Holy Island and the author of several books on Celtic spirituality. The extracts I have chosen are his own compositions taken from his book *The Edge of Glory*, published in 1985, and are reproduced with the kind permission of Triangle Books, SPCK.

The Carmina Gadelica is a collection of poems and prayers orally collected by Alexander Carmichael (born 1832) in the Highlands and islands of Scotland. The extracts I have chosen have been reproduced with the kind permission of the Scottish Academic Press.

The extract 'Iona, Iona, Iona' from *Columba, the Play with Music* by Juliet Boobbyer and Joanna Sciortino was taken from an anthology called *The Celtic Heart* and is quoted with permission of Gracewing (Fowler Wright Books Ltd).

D.H. Lawrence, 'Shadows': this much loved poem is reproduced from *The Complete Poems of D.H. Lawrence*, edited by V. de Sola Pinto and F.W. Roberts, copyright © 1964, 1971 by Angelo Ravagli and C.M. Weekley, executors of the

Estate of Frieda Lawrence Ravagli. Used by permission of the author's agent Laurence Pollinger Ltd and the Estate of Frieda Lawrence Ravagli, and in the USA by Viking Penguin, a division of Penguin Putnam Inc. Grateful thanks to Jack and Susan Schmidt of Cincinnati, Ohio, for their assistance.

Extracts from G.R.D. McLean's work, *Praying with Highland Christians*, published in 1988 and 1996, are reproduced with the kind permission of Triangle Books, SPCK. Traditional Gaelic poems and prayers were collected from all over the Highlands (originally collected by Alexander Carmichael for the *Carmina Gadelica*) and McLean put a selection of these into modern verse for English readers. The origins of the poems and prayers go back at least to the seventeenth century, and elements of them are certainly more ancient than that.

Caroline Moore has kindly given permission for the use of two prayers written by her for use in St Aidan's Chapel in Bradford Cathedral.

Alison Newell's prayer, 'Let the flowers close', is taken from *The Iona Community Worship Book*, published in 1991, and is used by permission of Wild Goose Publications, Glasgow.

George Sigerson's translation of the prayer *'Deus meus adiuva me'* (from the eighteenth-century *Bards of the Gael and Gall*) is published in *A Celtic Anthology* by Grace Rhys, published by George G. Harrap & Co. Ltd, 1927.

R.S. Thomas' poem 'The Bright Field' was taken from *Laboratories of the Spirit*, published by Macmillan in 1975.

SOURCES AND ACKNOWLEDGEMENTS

Rev. Robert Van de Weyer is the founder of the Community of Christ the Sower based at Little Gidding. He is currently priest of four rural parishes. Extracts from his book *Letters of Pelagius* are reproduced with his kind permission.

Cornish sources
The Companions of St Guenole is an ecumenical movement which came into being in 1987 as a result of the friendship between the late Rt Rev. Peter Mumford and Abbé Jean de la Croix of the monastery at Landevennec in Brittany. In celebrating their Celtic roots Christians of all denominations are able to bridge the divide that separates them today, for, in the words of Jean de la Croix in his sermon at the Towednack pilgrimage in 1987, 'We've been together for longer than we've been apart.'

The Cornish Ordinalia is a trilogy of religious drama, namely 'Origo Mundi', 'Passio Domini', and 'Resurrexio Domini'. Along with *Beunans Meriasek*, the work was almost certainly composed at Glasney College, Penryn, during the late fourteenth century and was performed in open-air theatres. The early translations of both works are held by the Royal Institute of Cornwall in Truro. The translations used in this collection have been produced by the Cornish Language Board and are reproduced with their kind permission.

Perran Gay is Canon Chancellor of the Diocese of Truro and his hymn 'Father God, your love surrounds us' is reproduced with his kind permission.

Gormola Kernewek (Cornish Praise) is a collection of poems and prayers composed by the author.

Anne Ham is a Cornish-based poet and has kindly given permission for use of part of her poem 'In the stillness of the night'.

John Harris was born at Bolenowe near Camborne in Cornwall in 1820. He was a tin miner, as was his father before him, and he spent most of his youth in the blackness of the mines. In contrast his poetry is brimming with colour and detail. It is the work of a man who delights in the light and who sees God in all of Creation. The poems were published by John Harris during the latter part of the nineteenth century, along with *My Autobiography*, and have been more recently republished by Donald M. Thomas in his book *Songs from the Earth: Selected Poems of John Harris, Cornish Miner 1820–84* (Padstow: Lodenek Press, 1977), and by Paul Newman in his book *Meads of Love* (Dyllansow Truran, 1994).

Robert Hawker DD was vicar of Plymouth and father to the more well known eccentric Parson Hawker of Morwenstow in Cornwall. Poems and other writings from both father and son are included in this anthology. Those by Robert Hawker are taken from *Morning Portion*, published in 1836 by Frederick Westley and A.A. Davis, and from *Evening Portion*, published in 1837 by Simpkin Marshall & Co. Those by Parson Hawker of Morwenstow can be found in *The Poetical Works of R.S. Hawker*, published by The Bodley Head in 1867, and in *Hawker of Morwenstow* by Piers Brendon, published by Jonathan Cape in 1975.

Mark Guy Pearse was born in Camborne in 1842. He was a Methodist minister and a prolific writer of sermons, homilies and poetry. He died in 1929. Writings included in this anthology are taken from *Some Aspects of a Blessed Life*, published by T. Woolmer in 1880, and *Come Break Your Fast*, published in 1897 by S.W. Partridge & Co.

SOURCES AND ACKNOWLEDGEMENTS

Paul Randall-Morris is a Cornish poet and the poems I have used have been taken with his kind permission from *Poems from the Heart* and *A Word or Two*, first published in 1994.

Bernard Walke of St Hilary, Cornwall, wrote *Bethlehem: A Christmas Play*, assisted by Annie Walke and Rev. Malton, published by Methuen and Co. Ltd in 1936.

If any required acknowledgements have been omitted or any rights overlooked we would ask those concerned to notify the publishers, who will be happy to include any further details in future reprints.

The author would also like to express her grateful thanks to Mrs Eunice Ross and Mrs Susan Pearce for typing the original scripts and for their continued encouragement.

INTRODUCTION

The Celtic saints lived at a time when Christianity was still new, fresh as the morning dew. To these remarkable men and women God was the infinite power of creation, the great High King of Heaven whose dealings with mankind, revealed by a loving Christ, showed a gentleness and compassion that were almost beyond comprehension. It was this combination of strength and gentleness that the Celtic saints strove to emulate in their own lives.

They lived in a harsh environment and were often afraid, but as we look back, their serenity and their conviction shame us. We lack their urgency, their fire, their steadfastness of faith. Where we stumble, they walked sure footed. Yet many of us are descended from this vigorous, prolific race. Their blood courses in our veins and the spark that lit them has the power to light us too. In the prayers the Celtic saints left behind, this light shines brightly, and that same light is a gleaming thread in other prayers, poems and translations that have come to us through the ages, without beginning and without end. In true Celtic style the love of a saving Christ is woven like an intricate pattern into the very fabric of all our lives.

I have tried to show how the gospel came to the western shores of Britain and how the various influences came together to form what has become known as 'Celtic Christian spirituality'. Essentially it is a story of men and women afire with the spirit of the living God. Cameos of the saints' lives head each section, and the poems and prayers have been drawn from sources that span nearly two thousand years.

As the millennium approaches, Celtic Christian spirituality is still a vibrant force. It has never become fixed in time or slipped into irrelevancy. The great High King of Heaven, the awesome creator of a universe beautiful beyond comprehension is, above all, seen to be ever-present in the simple, everyday things of life. The thrill of this peculiarly Celtic form of Christianity is that we can all be caught up in the very act of creation itself. The simple, everyday things of life become sanctified if we do them with joy in our hearts. And if we open our hearts to others, Jesus Christ, the son of the living God, will walk with us every step along the way.

1

A CELTIC LAND

WHEN the first wave of Celts trekked across Europe to settle in Britain they found a land sparsely inhabited by peaceful farmers who were struggling to eke out a living from the land and whose culture, once impressive, was now in decline.

For many centuries the star-worshipping people of the Stone Age had roamed the countryside and megalithic builders had built stone chambers in the earth, wombs of the Mother Goddess, whose mysteries were pierced once a year by the rays of the rising sun on the day of the winter solstice. These early races had in their turn made way for the more sophisticated workers in bronze. The 'Beaker' people arrived in Britain around 2400 BC and left behind them vast stone monuments of intricate mathematical and astronomical design. Other merchants and speculators travelled from Brittany in search of tin and copper, and they became both successful and wealthy, forming what is known to archaeologists as the 'Wessex culture'.

By 1400 BC, however, two not unconnected events resulted in disaster. The colossal eruption of the volcanic island of Thera in the Aegean Sea caused tidal waves which decimated the trading fleets of the Cretan sea kings. Overnight the miners and traders of Britain lost their major customers and suddenly, to add to their troubles, the British climate deteriorated. The debris from the volcano caused significant climatic changes throughout the world and Britain, in particular, became considerably wetter and cooler. The farmers of Britain were thrown into confusion. With the loss of familiar crops, the economy weakened quickly and the Wessex culture collapsed. The old religion, with its stone circles, menhirs and henges, was abandoned. The advanced astronomical and mathematical knowledge was forgotten and it was as if the whole of British society in the Bronze Age took a backward step. There followed years of poverty and decline. Although the people learnt to adapt to their new situation, the economy did not recover. The old prosperity and thriving culture were gone.

The first wave of Celts arrived in Britain during the eighth century BC, having travelled from the Hallstatt region of Austria. The wealth of these people in their homeland was based on salt mining. They were tall, powerful, clannish people who made great use of iron and they came to Britain in search of metal ores. Their arrival was unchallenged and heralded the beginning of the Iron Age in Britain. Large concentrations of iron were to be found in the Weald of Kent, and in

Cornwall the old copper and tin workings were discovered. Cornwall quickly became the focal point of Celtic activity, with the lode-bearing areas being rapidly ringed by fortresses for protection. These people, known as the 'Iron Age A' or 'Hallstatt culture', left very little of themselves for us to discover. They were mine workers and traders who had little time for the finer trappings of life. It was the later wave of Celts, who arrived in Britain around 400 BC from the La Teine region of Switzerland, who made the far greater impression. The 'La Teine culture', or 'Iron Age B' people were flamboyant and aggressive. They were skilled horse-riders, farmers, mariners, craftsmen and warriors who made good use of iron, bronze and tin, but whose greatest love was for their cattle and their gold. They journeyed in all directions from their homeland in search of new places to settle. They became known variously as the Keltoi, the Celts, the Galatians, or the Gauls, and their influence in Europe and the Near East was considerable.

These new arrivals in Britain reinforced the massive earthen ramparts of the ancient hill forts, many of which were large enough to hold the livestock they so prized and to provide protection for a thriving community. These hill forts were religious centres as well as being defensive enclosures, and within many of them craft work and the production of goods also took place. From them the chief of the tribe would hold sway over large tracts of surrounding land. Indigenous peoples were enslaved. By the first century BC the whole of Britain was divided into 33 Celtic tribal regions, each with their own craft workers, coinage and tribal ruler. Many village enclosures or rounds were built and the land was rigorously worked. The fortunes of Britain were once again in the ascendant.

The Celts were tall, well-built people. During the first century BC the Sicilian–Greek historian Diodorus Siculus wrote that '... their hair is blonde but not naturally so: they bleach it by washing it in lime and combing it back from their foreheads ... thick and shaggy like a horse's mane,' to present an awesome appearance in battle. Although many were in fact naturally blonde, dark- and red-headed Celts were just as common. Both men and women wore their hair long and the men had beards and heavy moustaches.

Their brightly coloured clothes reflected their flamboyant personalities. Heavily woven materials with intricate patterns were favoured by both men and women. The men wore trousers with drawstrings at the waist and ankle, along with a round-necked tunic and a woollen, calf-length cloak fastened at the shoulder with a beautifully fashioned brooch. Women wore long dresses belted at the waist, with similar cloaks to the men. Their hair was often plaited or coiled and held in position with a bronze pin.

The Celtic people loved their jewellery and it is this that has survived the passing of time to give us clues to their character and skills. Wristlets, armlets, torcs and brooches superbly made of bronze and gold, sometimes inlaid with coloured enamel and decorated with beautiful, flowing curves and circles, have all been found in ancient graves along with mirrors, combs, helmets, shields and swords. Celtic swords were iron-bladed with bronze hilts, strong and heavy like the men who wielded them, and each was named and regarded as a personal friend. For a Celtic warrior who was frequently called upon to defend his tribal lands or plunder others, his sword was sometimes his only friend.

From the earliest times the people of Europe had venerated the Goddess or Earth Mother, and to the Celts she was still the foundation of their belief system and their complicated family of gods. The Goddess was the Giver of Birth, symbolizing fertility and plenty. She was also known as Artemis, Venus, Anna, Diana, and in Ireland as Bridget or Bride.

Lord of all the animals was Cernunnos, the Horned God, who was seen by the Celts as the ruler of the natural kingdom and lord of the underworld. Among the other many gods were Dagda the Good Father, Belenos the sun-god, Taranis the Thunderer, Morrigan the war goddess and Teutatos the protector of people. The animals had their protectors too, such as Epona the horse goddess, from whose name we get our word 'pony'.

Controlling this world of gods and people were the awesome Celtic priests or Druids. The Druids came exclusively from the warrior classes and to attain their priesthood they had to undertake some twenty years of gruelling periods of instruction. Nothing was written down. Rituals and wisdom had to be remembered and handed down to succeeding generations by word of mouth. The Druids were wise men, seers and the officials of rituals. They were feared and respected. They were also experts at the art of divining, and the entrails of sacrificed slaves or animals were examined for auspices of the future.

One ritual that has made its mark on the minds of the British people is that of the Young King or Green Man. Each New Year a young man was chosen to be 'king'. For one full year he could indulge himself in all the pleasures of life, but when the year drew to a close he would be drugged with mead and ceremonially killed by being forced to sit on the sharpened stump of a young thorn tree. As the body decayed, so the tree would continue to grow and before long, new shoots would be seen sprouting from mouth, ear and nose sockets. It was intended to be a continual reminder to the people of the perpetual cycle of life and death, and it has indeed proved to be a most powerful symbol, remembered down through the generations to the present day. But this annual ceremony, along with that of the burning of a live man in a wicker basket, although long remembered, may be remnants of an older religion and not attributable to the era of the Celts.

There seems no doubt, however, that human and animal sacrifice did often form a major part in Druidic ceremonies and that the Druids themselves were as much feared as they were respected. The Druids alone were believed to have the power to summon the gods and harness their power. The Druids also had the power to disappear and reappear at will and to 'shape-shift', or to materialize in other living forms. A Druid's curse or blessing was powerful indeed and places sacred to the Druids – the groves and high places, oak and yew trees, caves and lakes – were much revered. When a Druid summoned the people, they came.

The Celtic year was divided into four seasons, with festivals held on the first day of each season. *Samhain* (1 November to 31 January) was the Celtic New Year. On the eve of 1 November, the veil between earth and heaven was believed to be at its thinnest and as the sun sank and the dark deepened, so the dead streamed across the gulf of Annwn on a bridge of swords and walked on earth again. All across Britain people left out food and drink for their returning loved ones. During the days preceding Samhain the stock were brought in from the hills and the weak animals who would be unable to survive the winter ahead were killed, their flesh salted, their skins preserved and the bones boiled. At midnight on Samhain Eve great fires were lit from a sacred flame tended by the Druids. These fires would burn until morning. Bonfires – or bonefires – on which the unwanted carcasses of the slaughtered animals would be burnt to dust, were lit on high places and the embers from these fires were taken back to people's homes to be rekindled in their hearths.

During the season of Samhain came the winter solstice, on 21 December. On this day prayers were made to the gods that they would not abandon the earth to the great darkness. In the bleakest of winters these prayers often seemed like pleas of despair and the need for greater sacrifices must have seemed imperative. Among the peasant people of Britain were those who had distant memories of past ceremonies involving the megalithic chambers of the Mother Goddess, and small groups would gather to watch the rays of the rising sun pierce the gloom of her underground womb to fertilize the earth once more.

The season of *Imbolc* (1 February to 30 April) was dedicated to the Goddess. Newborn lambs and young girls would jump through burning hoops of plaited straw to invoke her powers of fertility, and babies born during November were known by all to be children of Imbolc. Winter still enveloped the world, but signs of spring were becoming evident and it was a time of hope, a time to make plans.

The season of *Beltane* (1 May to 31 July) was also marked by fire. It was the festival of the Sun and great bonfires were lit on the hill tops and at other sacred places in Britain, two fires to each site. It was a joyous time marking the beginning of summer. Clothes were washed, homes were swept clean and old straw bedding was taken to be burnt on the fires. The kitchen fires which had burnt throughout the winter went unfed during the day and the embers were raked out. As dusk fell, all fires and lights were extinguished and darkness reigned as the villagers climbed the hills and gathered around the two beacon fires. This period of darkness was a time to be careful, for it was a time when witches and evil spirits were thought be abroad. When the night was at its darkest, the fire of Beltane was kindled and, as the bonfires blazed into the night sky, the people would take up the chant of Beltane. A goat was sacrificed and its body thrown on the fire. The people gathered their livestock and drove them between the two great fires to protect them from disease. Then was the time for feasting and merriment. The cows were decorated with collars of straw and the young girls were given garlands of flowers. Fire was taken from the bonfires and distributed to the houses to relight the kitchen fires, and then feasting and dancing, drinking and games began in earnest and would continue all night until the people collapsed in exhaustion. Summer had begun.

The last of the seasons was *Lughnasa* (1 August to 31 October), the time of harvest, and the festival that heralded its beginning was held in honour of ferocious Lug, the god of hard work and bravery in battle. It was an anxious time because life and death depended on the harvest. The land boundaries had to be patrolled to protect the harvest from raiders. The Mother Goddess was beseeched and Lug was brought gifts so that they would intercede on behalf of the people. At every vagary of the weather, gifts from the various crafts were offered, and votive dances which mimed the occupations of the people were performed until the dancers worked themselves into a frenzy and dropped with exhaustion. When a good harvest had been safely gathered in at last, and next year's seed had been stored, there was an enormous sense of relief, for this was a society close to the earth. The weather, the harvest and the recurring seasons were woven into the very fabric of their lives.

The image of the Iron-Age Celts as savage, primitive, woad-painting Ancient Britons is not an accurate one. The remains of their civilization show that they were an advanced, tenacious and hard-working people. Their personality was quickly stamped on the land and the smaller, less aggressive races of indigenous people were soon absorbed or enslaved by the new arrivals. Cattle-rearing, agriculture and the mining of precious ores were still the major occupations. Trading links with Europe, and particularly with the lands of the Mediterranean, were forged and routes linking customers and traders were opened. For a couple of centuries Britain became part of a Pan-Celtic culture and, although life was harsh and basic, on the whole it was orderly and held every potential for prosperity.

But just as the Celts had once swarmed across Europe in search of new lands, now a more disciplined force threatened to do the same. During the first century BC armies from Rome started marching north, and bit by bit large tracts of land and the fierce Celtic tribes were subdued by their might. In 55 and 54 BC Julius Caesar crossed the Channel with his army, but he was beaten off and it was left to Claudius and Vespasian to invade Britain. From AD 43 until AD 410 Britain became part of the Roman Empire and Roman rule held sway over the eastern and southern part of the island. Separated by the mass of Dartmoor, however, the Romans made little impression in the west. The only Romans the people of Cornwall are likely to have seen were the occasional trader or teacher. The Romans made no serious effort to subdue the west of the country and the Iron Age continued in the western fringes of Britain until the end of the fourth century AD.

2

FIRE FROM THE EAST

SKIRTING around the fringes of the mighty Roman Empire, the merchants and sea traders of the Mediterranean took scant notice of the politics of the day. They were the entrepreneurs, the adventurers. There were fortunes to be made. Navigating by the stars and hugging the rugged coasts of Spain and France, sturdy wooden ships travelled the ancient sea routes, laden with oil, wine, grain and barrels of salt, with their red-brown sails bulging in the strong winds. Long before the Roman armies crossed into eastern Britain, merchant ships from the Levant had landed in Cornwall, Wales and southern Ireland in search of new enterprise – tin and silver from Cornwall and gold from Wales and Ireland.

These were much prized cargoes. They were well worth the risk of the long, treacherous journey and many a rich merchant from the East made the trip alongside their sea-hardened crews in order to seek out new contracts and sweeten old ones. Local chieftains, greedy for wealth, used slave labour, snatched from neighbouring communities, to ensure that a steady supply of tin, silver and gold reached the shores ready to be exchanged when the ships arrived. The little town of Marazion (Jew's Market) in Cornwall was a favoured trading port where ships from the Mediterranean would drop anchor and find shelter in the calm of the bay. Under the shadow of St Michael's Mount, tin (hacked from the living rock at Ding Dong) would be hustled on board the impatient fleet of small vessels. Lines of men, bent double by the weight of barrel and sack, would scurry to and fro between shore and hill-top fort. Trade was all-important.

Cornwall is a land of mist and mystery, where legends abound. When holidaying in Cornwall at the end of the eighteenth century, William Blake heard the ancient and much loved story that Joseph of Arimathea had come to Cornwall aboard one of his merchant ships and brought with him the child Jesus. Blake was so moved by the idea that when he returned home he was inspired to write the now famous words of his poem 'Jerusalem':

> And did those feet in ancient time
> Walk upon England's mountains green?
> And was the holy Lamb of God
> On England's pleasant pastures seen?

Did the Christ-child really walk in Cornwall? We shall probably never know. But what we do know is that ships bring news. Wherever they dock local people gather, avid for news. Gossip and scandal and dreams spread like wildfire.

It was not long before stories of despotic emperors and persecutions reached the shores of Britain. Stories too of a new faith, a triumph of life over death, of good over evil. Stories of a people on fire with excitement, preparing themselves for the return to earth of a risen Lord.

It was to be many years before the Christianity embraced by the Roman world would travel overland to reach these western regions. The first taste of this new faith for the people of Cornwall, Wales, Ireland and the west coast of Scotland came by sea from the East, probably within the first hundred years AD, to be reinforced in the fourth century by the migration of large numbers of Latin-speaking Christians from Gaul.

In a Roman world these Christians from Gaul were something of an anomaly. Influenced by the teachings of the Eastern Fathers and encouraged by Martin of Tours, they were inspired to seek some 'desert' place for solitary contemplation and worship. The mysticism and asceticism of Eastern Christianity was distinctly foreign to the Roman Church in France. Those who accepted these ideas, and put them into practice, found a spirit of marked hostility developing towards them in Gaulish Episcopal circles.

In their great desire and determination to seek a place to be free to worship as they wished, they left their homes and migrated west and north, finally settling in widely scattered communities in Brittany, Cornwall, Wales, the Isle of Man, Ireland and Scotland. The Iron-Age people of Britain were less sophisticated and conditions were harsher than those to which these early Christians were accustomed. Many of them were killed, but huddling together in small communities, and trusting in the strength of Christ, some survived. Evidence of their settlement in these places is found in the large number of Christian stone monuments inscribed in Latin which are scattered throughout the region.

Influenced by the stories of the eastern sea traders and impressed by the lives of these early Christians from Gaul, the fire which first ignited the souls of the Celtic people of western Britain was without doubt fire from the East. The teachings of the Eastern Fathers gleam like strands of light through all the surviving Celtic literature.

Too often in our modern eyes the Fathers of the Eastern Church remain shadowy and mysterious, their names forgotten, their long battles with emperors and heretics remembered only as footnotes, their works gathering dust. Yet, as we look back, the urgency of their message, the serenity and certainty of their faith, the brilliance in their eyes and their fine-spun imaginations lit with the orient sun come down to us through the ages with a freshness that is startling to the modern Western mind.

Yet it struck a chord in the minds of the people of the western regions of Britain – a chord that is still resounding. And it was the teaching of these Eastern Fathers that so inspired St Martin of Tours, who befriended the young Bishop Ninian in AD 394, and who encouraged these Christians from Gaul to venture out to the western lands of Britain. Martin, a Hungarian by nationality and an officer in the Roman army, was at Amiens in France in AD 337 when a semi-naked beggar approached him in bitterly cold weather. According to tradition, Martin took his sword and cut his military cloak in two, giving half to the shivering man. For this generous but foolhardy action Martin received a fair amount of ribbing from his companions, but that night he had a dream. In this dream he saw Christ, dressed in the half-cloak, talking to his disciples, and he heard Christ say, 'See what a fine cloak Martin gave me today.'

Martin left the army and joined the Church, longing to be a hermit and to seek Christ in the desert places. Instead, the Church in its wisdom made him a bishop. Unable to live as he wished, Martin encouraged others to seek Christ in solitude and, inspired by his dream, he taught his followers to see Christ in the faces of those around them, in both friend and stranger.

His charismatic personality and his vision drew hundreds of young people to him at Tours, all eager to become monastics, all eager to seek Christ in the desert places of the world. From among this number came fervent young settlers to the western shores of Britain. They came in search of a desert place and found wild sea coasts and swirling mists, woodland groves and craggy peaks. And in every lark that sang, in every face they met, they found their sweet Lord.

Living in caves or beehive huts near natural springs and often hidden away from their unpredictably fierce neighbours, these Christian travellers gradually settled into the areas of the West Country. Their sense of discipline and their need to purge themselves with severe deprivations following the example of the Eastern Fathers set them apart from their neighbours, but slowly they came to be trusted. Their behaviour marked them as holy men and as such they were revered, for the Celts believed, as did most civilizations of the time, that the mad and the holy of all races must be protected. When these young men stood up to their necks in cold water reciting aloud psalm after psalm for hours and sometimes days on end, the local population must have wondered where madness ended and holiness began!

The writings favoured by these early Christians were those favoured by the Eastern Fathers: the Gospels of John and Thomas, the Psalms and Athanasius' *Life of St Antony of Egypt*. The calendar of festivals they chose to follow was that of the Eastern Church and not that of Rome. Theirs was a harsh and simple life, but every moment was shared with their Lord. Jesus walked with them on the road and in His pathway they walked in fear and trembling. They saw Him in the face of friend and stranger, in the flight of white birds, beside them on every path. To Eastern Father and Christian pilgrim alike, sanctity dwelt in all things. All that was made by God, all that was touched by

His hand, was holy. The stars were sacred, and so were spiders' webs, so were grasses waving in the wind. Man, too, was sacred, for did he not possess a body capable of resurrection and transfiguration? Holiness was all around – a tangible something you could almost gather in your hands.

How these young idealists from Gaul survived among the boisterous, warlike Celts of western Britain has to be a mystery of faith, but survive they did. They survived because they too were Celts and, although they came from a more sophisticated region, they shared the Celtic heart.

We do not have much in the way of writings from this time, but the same sense of the power of God, His protection for His people, the wonders of His creation, His presence in friend and stranger, can be seen in the hymns traditionally ascribed to St Patrick.

St Patrick was born in AD 389 in Bannavem, which is thought to have been a coastal village in north-west England. Brought up in a Christian home, Patrick was captured by an Irish raiding party and taken away to Ireland. There he worked as a slave, tending sheep and pigs and looking for a chance to escape. Six years later his opportunity came and he sailed home. But his experience had left him unsettled and he returned to Ireland determined to spread the word of God among its people. He made his way to Tara, the centre of Druidic worship and witchcraft, and his arrival coincided with the festival of Beltane during which all lights had to be put out and all fires extinguished.

As darkness fell, Patrick determined to show the light of Christ in this heathen place and he climbed the beacon hill and lit the huge fire which was visible for miles around. The King ordered his soldiers to search out and kill the man who had lit the fire too early, but Patrick escaped and, because he came to no harm and was protected by his God, the people of Ireland began to question the power of the Druids.

This poem attributed to St Patrick may have been contemporary to the event:

> At Tara today in this fateful hour
> I place all heaven within its power
> And the sun with its brightness
> And the snow with its whiteness
> And the fire with all the strength it hath,
> And lightning with its rapid wrath,
> And the winds with their swiftness along their path,
> And the sea with its deepness,
> And the earth with its starkness:
> All these I place,
> By God's almighty grace,
> Between myself and the powers of darkness.

The poem known as 'St Patrick's Breastplate' may have been written many years after his death, but the sentiments are those of this early period of Celtic Christianity, full of fire and wonder and paradox, and many of the sentiments of the Eastern Fathers can be traced in its writing (see pages 109–12).

Using the ancient seaways to keep in contact, these early Christians encouraged each other to remain constant. Letters and manuscripts and the occasional visiting monk came to them from the East, and even the much revered Jerome wrote to them, giving them confidence in their solitude and doing much to renew their vision. Small communities were established, some of which flourished to become centres of learning and spiritual growth.

All around them the people of Iron-Age Britain lived their lives, the trading continued and warring chieftains regularly summoned their men to pillage and raid their neighbours' territories. More and more people were, however, leaving the hill-top forts and making their dwellings in less inhospitable settings. The influence of the traders and merchant seamen with their knowledge of other civilizations was beginning to make its mark. But still it was a harsh environment and it was the remarkable faith of these isolated groups of early Christians that kept the flame of Christianity alive in the western districts. Their God was all-powerful. He lived within them. He lived without them. If they drew a *caim*, or circle, around themselves each day and invoked His protection, they had nothing to fear.

3

CONFLICT

AWAY from the western regions, Roman civilization took firm hold of Britain in the early centuries AD. On 27 August 55 BC, Roman troops led by Julius Caesar, the conqueror of Gaul, landed on British soil for the first time. After a fierce struggle 10,000 men of the Seventh and Tenth Legions secured a foothold on the beach between Deal and Walmer on the Kent coast, but their position was untenable, surrounded as they were by wild Celtic warriors. Recognizing the strength of the opposition, Caesar quickly set about negotiating a truce with the local tribes. This held for less than three weeks until the British tribes, deciding that after all they stood a good chance of ridding themselves of the Roman force, attacked again, this time with cavalry and chariots. The Romans held their ground and the British retreated to regroup. Then the weather deteriorated and Caesar, knowing that he was in a difficult position and could not expect help from the continent, slipped quietly away under cover of darkness.

During the summer of 54 BC he returned with five legions, 800 ships and 2,000 cavalry. This time they were more successful and penetrated the British defences as far as present-day Colchester. When they returned to Gaul in the autumn they left behind them a number of Celtic–British leaders in the pay of Rome. So even though the Romans themselves had gone, their influence was still felt, and trading with Roman-occupied countries on the continent began to flourish.

It was not until the summer of AD 43 that the Romans returned in earnest with 200,000 men, but even then it took 40 years to subdue the Celtic–British tribes. But subdue them they did, one by one, until all but the far north of Scotland and the western fringes of Britain were brought firmly under Roman rule. For three and a half centuries, until the armies were recalled to Rome in AD 401 to help defend that beleaguered city against attacks from the Germanic Barbarians, Britain belonged to Rome. It became part of a vast Roman Empire stretching from the Persian Gulf to the Western Sea.

As the leaders of the Celtic tribes sued for peace one by one, it became the duty of the Roman governors to restore control and introduce Roman rule and Roman civilization. New roads and towns were built. New temples to new gods were erected and leading British families were quick to appreciate the comparative luxuries of Roman life. The ambitious swiftly mastered Latin and grasped every opportunity to find new avenues of trade. The living conditions of the British middle class improved considerably as they strove to emulate the life of their Roman overlords.

In matters of religion the Romans showed pragmatic tolerance and allowed the worship of Celtic gods to carry on alongside worship of the Roman deities. A superstitious race, they were not anxious to incur the displeasure of a slighted god.

Christianity came to Britain with the Roman families and small shrines have been found in private houses belonging to this time. Although the numbers of Christians were growing rapidly, they were not in any way organized and they were not well understood by most people. They were often thought of as being subversive as they refused to honour the cult of the Emperor. Still, as long as they did not cause problems the Roman authorities tended to turn a blind eye to their activities, especially as large numbers of Roman families had at least one Christian convert in their ranks. Thus Christianity was making its mark in Roman-held Britain as well as becoming known from different sources in the country's western fringes.

In June of AD 208 a man from Verulamium (St Albans) is said to have hidden a Christian priest from the authorities. When the officers came to the house Albanus dressed in the priest's robes and surrendered in his place. He was tortured and put to death. In view of events like this, it was probably wiser for Christians to keep quiet about their beliefs.

In AD 312 all that changed. Before advancing into battle against the Italians, Emperor Constantine dreamt he saw the Chi Ro Christian symbol in the sky over the battlefield. On waking he ordered his soldiers to paint the symbol on their shields. His victory was stupendous and he vowed to acknowledge publicly the power of the Christian God. All of a sudden it became fashionable to be a Christian. Christian symbols began to adorn the floors of private villas. Sunday was observed as a holy day. Christian burial began to take the place of Celtic funeral pyres, and priests and bishops became respected members of the community.

In the country areas of Britain the peasants continued to observe the old feast days and worship the Celtic gods, but Christianity became the preferred religion of the town dwellers, the middle classes and those seeking preferment. On the continent the Christian Church became more organized and sophisticated, and it was during this period of fashionable Christianity that Martin of Tours struggled to bring his congregations back to the simplicity of the gospel and the ascetic way of life taught by the early Eastern Fathers. His disciples travelled west in order to live their simple Christian lives. A small group landed and settled in Kent, but a far larger number travelled until they reached the Celtic–British lands beyond the influence of Rome and were able to find the freedom they so desired.

In AD 391 Emperor Theodosius issued a decree outlawing pagan worship. The status of Christianity grew even greater as the worship of Celtic and the old Roman gods was driven underground.

For a few short years all but the western fringes of Britain formed part of a vast Christian Roman Empire. Road networks linked all the cities, large estates flourished, great buildings were constructed, watermills ground corn and a new professional class of doctors, lawyers, theologians, bishops, priests and merchants prospered in a well-ordered society. The Britons under Roman rule could well be called Romano-British, while those in the lands untouched by Roman occupation remained Celtic–British.

With the Roman armies in occupation, the people of Britain enjoyed a period of peace and prosperity. But suddenly, in AD 401 and without warning, the legions in Britain were withdrawn to Rome and the unprotected British shores were left wide open to attack. On the continent swarms of people were on the move looking for land. In AD 410 Emperor Honorius wrote to tell the Britons that they must fight the 'barbarians' that threatened them without help from Rome. This was a bitter blow. Already demoralized by Roman withdrawal, the citizens of some eastern coastal towns abandoned their homes for fear of invasion by Saxon hordes and in desperation German mercenaries were employed to keep the enemy out.

Gradually, however, wave upon wave of the new settlers invaded British shores. Angles, Saxons and Jutes met little resistance and the newcomers made their homes where they wished. Many Romano-British people kept their heads down and reluctantly accepted these invaders as neighbours. Others fled west and gathered together with the Celtic Britons in Dumnonia and Wales, making independent forays behind the Saxon lines.

During this period the British-born theologian Pelagius, not very aware of what was happening in the land of his birth, was making his ideas known in Palestine. Pelagius was a fine debater and his views mirrored those of his fellow Christians in Ireland. Pelagius believed that everyone could choose whether or not to sin. This doctrine of free will was at odds with the mainstream Church whose bishops preached that no one could escape 'original sin' without the grace of God. But Pelagius believed that when God created man He created him without sin. The influence of the Eastern Fathers and joy in the 'goodness' of creation was a message well learnt in the fringes of western Britain, and Pelagius' teaching was widely accepted. But such Church worthies as St Augustine of Hippo and Jerome combined with the authorities to condemn what they called 'Pelagianism' out of hand. In AD 429 Bishop Germanus of Auxerre was sent to Britain to counter this heresy and stamp it out entirely. He was quite successful in his mission, but many Celtic–British Christians, now joined by the migrating Romano-British Christians, were beyond his reach in the valleys of Wales, the wilds of Cornwall or the island fortress of Ireland, and their defiant 'Pelagian' views continued unabated.

St Patrick, born near Carlisle, and a crucial figure in Celtic Christian history, was brought up in the traditions of the Roman Church, but when he was later made Bishop of Ireland he became much influenced by the teachings of the Celts. Although he was often at odds with these stubborn, independent men and women, like most successful leaders he capitalized on what was good in their customs and teachings and built on it.

Early Romano-Christianity, with its sense of duty, order and diplomacy, and early Celtic Christianity, with its fiery independence, austerity and love of the desert places, seem unlikely bed-fellows. But thrown together as they were by the invasion of the Saxons, these two very different strands of Christianity entwined in their mutual love of a saving Lord Jesus. Together they flourished. In Ireland, Wales and Scotland, with the valleys of Wales in particular becoming the heart of this fusion of Christian strands, monasteries and places of learning were quickly established. The Scriptures were studied and young men were trained as missionaries, and for the next two centuries the Celtic Christian Church in western Britain was a powerful and organized entity, disciplined yet enthusiastic.

Following in the footsteps of the great founders, Ninian in Scotland, Patrick in Ireland, Dyfed in Wales and Columba on Iona, there arose among them three orders of saints or holy men and women. First there were the bishops, who possessed a roving commission rather than a territorial one, then the abbots, who were in charge of the monastic houses, and finally the *peregrini*, or wandering saints, who roamed the lands and seas in search of a desert place where they could live and spend their lives in prayer, praise and meditation. For these

Celtic Christians their lives were ones of martyrdom: a green martyrdom for the Christian who denied him- or herself the comforts of life, a white martyrdom for those who left home and family behind, and a red martyrdom for those who gave their lives for their faith.

For the *peregrini* travelling in small coracles across treacherous seas, carrying only their staff, bell and altar stone, the white martyrdom was theirs. The white cross of Christ blazoned against the blackness of the world's evil became their emblem. Wherever they stopped and stayed for a while they would set up one or two beehive cells and possibly a wooden preaching cross. In time the saint would move on, but the place would remain holy and a small, wattle-and-daub church would be built retaining the name of its founder. These wandering holy men criss-crossed the western lands of Britain and France, so that today villages, towns and churches can be found bearing the same name in Brittany, Cornwall, Ireland and Wales – all pointing to the intrepid voyaging of these fervent missionary saints. As they travelled they discovered many small cells of Christians founded by the first wave of Martin's disciples struggling to survive, and they were able to engender fresh hope and with their sense of order re-establish Christian communities where discipline had become lax and where the fire of faith was flickering low.

For many years the Saxon advance through the country was held at bay by the British warriors, and stories of the battles that ensued have been glorified in the legends of King Arthur and his knights. But the

Saxon warlords advanced relentlessly, systematically and ruthlessly beating the British armies into the ground.

At Chester in AD 615 the Saxon armies of King Athelfrith marched to deal with the remaining British troops, only to find that 1,200 monks from the nearby monastery of Bangor-is-y-Coed were gathered on the mountainside praying for the British army. Athelfrith was furious and decided that the monks, by praying, were fighting in the only way they knew how and were therefore participants in the battle. He ordered his soldiers to attack them first. Monks and army were annihilated.

While the massacre of Christian monks was happening in the west of England, Saxons in the eastern areas were already being converted to Christianity. Sent by Pope Gregory, Augustine, a monk from Rome, came to Britain to preach Christianity to the Saxons and Angles. Augustine was an austere man who impressed many by the simplicity of his life, and Christianity began once more to take its hold on the land. Unfortunately Augustine was not by nature either diplomatic or compromising, and when he held two conferences near the River Severn in Gloucestershire and invited delegates from the Celtic churches to meet him there, he treated them arrogantly and they took offence, refusing to take part in the talks.

The Pope may have appointed Augustine as Bishop of Britain, but Augustine never lived to bring the whole of the country under his jurisdiction. The pagan Angles and Saxons accepted his message, but faced with the stubborn Celtic–British Christians in the west, he had to acknowledge defeat. They refused to accept his authority and they declined to alter their customs and bring them in line with the Church in Europe. They were determined to keep the Eastern Orthodox manner of calculating the date of Easter, and they preferred to keep their strange tonsure which had been inherited from the first disciples of Martin of Tours. No amount of cajoling, persuading or threatening would change them.

It was not until AD 664, when the Celtic bishops met with the Saxon bishops at Whitby and debated the whole issue, that the Celts were finally forced to agree to come into line with the Roman Church. The procedure was a painful one, but the Synod of Whitby nonetheless marked the beginning of the end for Celtic Christianity in Britain – or did it?

What was good and true in Celtic spirituality has never really died. The independent hearts of Celtic descendants everywhere still yearn for the solitary place, still rejoice in the goodness of creation, still see the Lord beside them as they walk, still see Him in the face of friend and stranger. The gospel light with its Eastern fire still gleams. The truth still lingers in the heart.

A CELTIC
ANTHOLOGY

4

ST PIRAN

The lives of many of the *peregrini*, or wandering saints, have been much dramatized over the years, and wonderful, often amusing, miracles have been attributed to them. Many have been adopted and held in great affection as patron saints because of some particular incident which has lived on in legend. St Piran, the patron saint of Cornwall and the tin miners, is one such. This traditional poem illustrates the marvellous fondness, mingled with irreverence, which is typical of the Celtic attitude to holy things, bound up so closely with the whole of their lives. Early Celtic saints are still often referred to in such familiar terms as 'good ol' man', or 'dear maid'.

> 'Tis the legend of old Perranzabuloe,
> On the Cornish coast where the sand-storms blow,

THE CELTIC HEART

In those good times of myth and of dream,
Of giant and pixy and Cornish cream,

The beautiful Duchy, I'm much afraid,
Had not many saints that were quite home-made.

St Piran himself, of blessed fame,
Sure 'twas from County Cork he came.

He lived in a time when the Irish folk
Thought breaking of heads was a capital joke.

Now Piran hadn't a word to say
'Gainst breaking a head in a casual way;

But at last things grew to a pass so bad
That he cried, 'Be aisy now – stop it, bedad!'

Said they, 'Begorra, an' what are ye sayin'? –
Och, but a saint should be afther his prayin'.

'But sure if it's marthyrdom ye would be at,
We are the bhoys to obleege ye in that.'

So they tied the saint to a millstone strong;
To the top of a hill they dragged him along.

ST PIRAN

'Ye'll be wishing bad luck to the dhrop,' said they;
'Go on wid your praichin' now – out in the say.'

They rolled the stone over the cliff so steep.
Down where the waters were cruel and deep;

But as soon as it touched on the top of the sea
It steadied and floated as nice as could be.

Said Piran, 'I'm shaking your dust from me shoes'
(Though never a shoe did the good man use).

'It's demaining to spake to sich blackguards,' he said;
So he turned to a drop of the crayter instead.

(For he'd wisely concealed in a fold of his vest
A choice little flask of the Irish best.)

'And sure 'tis to Cornwall I'm going to-day,
And wanting a something for sich a long way.'

Now when the crowd saw that the saint wasn't drowned,
But sailed on the millstone quite happy and sound,

Said they, ''Tis the howly man floats on a stone,'
And were straightway converted with many a groan,

The celtic heart

But Piran sailed on till he came to that bay
Where the sand-heaps are drifting about to this day.

And with such little Latin as Piran did know
He said, '*This is Piran-in-sabulo.*'

He got off his millstone and murmured a grace;
And 'Arrah,' he said, ''tis an iligant place.

'A little too much o' the sand, maybe,
And a little too much o' the wet,' said he.

''Tis murther thrying to find one's way;
I'm almost wishing I'd stopped at say.'

And so he walked and wandered and ran,
Till he came to a hermit Cornishman.

He wished him most kindly the top of the day:
''Troth, I'm St Piran from over the way.

'You're a dacent bhoy,' said the saint most sweetly,
'And a howly man,' he added discreetly.

'I'm only axing a sup and a bite,
And a shake of straw for me bed the night.'

ST PIRAN

So the pair of saints hobnobbed together,
And grumbled a bit at the Cornish weather.

Said Piran, 'I've something to kape out the wet;
'Tis a dhrop of the Oirish best, me pet.'

But the Cornish saint looked a little awry
Out of the corner of his eye;

So he added, afraid of a wrong solution,
'I'm ordered a dhrop for me constitution;

''Tis not a biverage, sure, that I take,
But arrah, me health is so mortial wake.'

The Cornishman coughed, and then murmured, 'Aw well,
I reckon I'll try just a li'l bit mysel'.

'For I get the rheumatic so terrible bad.'
Said Piran, 'Rheumatic's the divel, me lad!'

They swallowed in turns so that bye-and-bye
The neat little flagon was quite drained dry.

The saint held it lovingly up to his lip;
'Bad cess to it thin, but I've had the last dhrip.

the celtic heart

'Niver mind, me riverend friend,' he said,
'It's me that knows how the crayter is made.'

They piled the stones that lay within reach,
And gathered the driftwood from off the beach;

And Piran said, 'If the powers be willin',
We'll do a nat little bit o' distillin'.'

The fire was lit and the barley was brought,
And St Piran did all that he had been taught.

But lo and behold, when the stones grew hot
A stream of white metal ran out on the spot.

Cried Piran, 'By all the powers, Amin!
Bedad if we haven't discovered Tin!

'Whirrish and whirroo! Me riverend brother,
How one good thing may lead to another!'

And that is why Piran, the truth to say,
Is the miners' saint to this very day.

(Traditional Cornish)

5

ST ANTONY

ST Antony was born in Egypt. His parents were rich and his life as a young man was comfortable and opulent. In AD 276 his parents died and Antony inherited all their wealth. Shortly after their death, he heard the story of Jesus telling the rich young man to sell all that he possessed and give it to the poor. Antony did not hesitate. He gave away all his possessions and retired almost immediately to the desert to live a life of solitude.

For more than twenty years Antony lived alone, often not seeing another human being for six months or more. He was frequently afraid, heard strange noises and was tempted by evil thoughts, but he strengthened himself with the belief that these were all the work of Satan who was trying to prevent him from being a servant of Jesus. Putting on the armour of Christ, he daily fought these beasts in the desert.

Although he desired nothing more than this solitary life alone with his Lord and Saviour, Antony attracted a large number of disciples. His life of discipline and holiness was seen as a model of the pure Christian life in contrast to the wickedness of the modern world. In AD 305 he reluctantly left his cell and founded a community of hermits who lived under rule, not in community but each in isolation. Five years later he returned to his cave, his reputation much enhanced. His name had become known throughout Christendom and from the desert he supported his friend Athanasius in his battle against the Arian heresy (i.e that Christ was not of one substance with the Father). Towards the end of his life the numbers of those turning to the solitary life increased dramatically. The Church itself was becoming wealthy and powerful and many were attracted by St Antony's contrastingly simple life.

Twenty years after Antony's death in AD 356, Martin of Tours in Gaul started to encourage his young followers to seek a desert place. *The Life of St Antony of Egypt* written by Athanasius was as well known to Christians in Gaul as was the Gospel of St John.

Antony's feast day is on 17 January.

Alone with God

Alone with none but you, my God,
I journey on my way.
What need I fear, when you are near,
O King of night and day?
More safe am I within your hand
Than if a host did round me stand.

My life I yield to your command,
And bow to your control,
In peaceful calm, for from your arm
No power can snatch my soul.
Could earthly foes ever appal
A soul that heeds the heavenly call?

(Attributed to St Columba, 6th century)

* * *

My robin, my lover, my dear
The sea is wonderful clear
The sky is so high
Yet my Saviour is nigh
Be still, for heaven is here.

(*Gormola Kernewek*, 20th century; written in
Mousehole, Cornwall, where 'my robin' is used
as term of endearment or greeting)

41

tbe celtic beart

Now
Robed in stillness
In this quiet place
Emptied of all that I am
Your gift of shepherding
to use and bless.

('Cuthbert's Prayer', by Caroline
Moore, for St Aidan's Chapel,
Bradford Cathedral, 20th century)

* * *

Shall I abandon, O King of Mysteries, the soft comforts of home? Shall I turn my back on my native land, and my face towards the sea?

Shall I put myself wholly at the mercy of God, without silver, without a horse, without fame and honour? Shall I throw myself wholly on the King of kings, without a sword and shield, without food and drink, without a bed to lie on?

Shall I say farewell to my beautiful land, placing myself under Christ's yoke? Shall I pour out my heart to him, confessing my manifold sins and begging forgiveness, tears streaming down my cheeks?

ST ANTONY

Shall I leave the prints of my knees on the sandy beach, a record of my final prayer in my native land? Shall I then suffer every kind of wound that the sea can inflict?

Shall I take my coracle across the wide, sparkling ocean? O King of the Glorious Heaven, shall I go of my own choice upon the sea?

O Christ, will you help me on the wild waves?

(St Brendan, 6th century)

* * *

Before prayer
I weave a silence onto my lips
I weave a silence into my mind
I weave a silence within my heart
I close my ears to distractions
I close my eyes to attractions
I close my heart to temptations.

Calm me O Lord as you stilled the storm
Still me O Lord, keep me from harm
Let all the tumult within me cease
Enfold me Lord in your peace.

(David Adam, *The Edge of Glory*, 20th century)

The Celtic Heart

A pleasant place I was at today,
under mantles of the worthy green hazel,
listening at day's beginning
to the skilful cock thrush
singing a splendid stanza
of fluent signs and symbols;
about him was a setting
of flowers of the sweet bough of May,
like green mantles, his chasuble
was the wings of the wind.
There was here, by the great God,
nothing but gold in the altar's canopy.
I heard, in polished language,
a long and faultless chanting,
an unhesitant reading to the people
of a gospel without mumbling;
the elevation, on the hill for us there,
of a good leaf for a holy wafer.
Then the slim eloquent nightingale
from the corner of a grove nearby,
poetess of the valley, sings to the many
the Sanctus bell in lively whistling.
The sacrifice is raised up to the sky above the bush,
devotion to God the Father,

ST ANTONY

the chalice of ecstasy and love.
The psalmody contents me:
it was bred of a birch-grove in the sweet woods.

(Dafydd ap Gwilym, 14th century)

* * *

And when the hush is deepest, and the moors
   Stretch away beneath the lofty sky,
Where quiet Evening folds her dusky doors,
   And on the marsh is heard the heron's cry,
No human face, no habitation nigh,
   Man, holding converse with his inner life,
Learns how to live, and better, how to die,
   And God Himself draws near to still the storm of strife.

(John Harris, *Monro*, 19th century)

τbe celτιc bearτ

He walk'd along, delighted with the world,
Delighted with himself, and all he met;
His eyes beheld, in everything around,
The Grandeur of the Highest. In the hill,
Golden with heather, he discover'd God;
In the rude rocks that ribb'd them, and the clouds
That gather'd on their summits, and the light
Which oped their revelation, clearly he
Saw God; and in the valleys shining, God;
In the dear wayside flowers, and narrow rills,
The trees, and shrubs, mosses, and blades of grass,
And humming bees, and sporting butterflies,
And white sand-grains along the sea-shore, God;
Above, below, and all around him, God.

(John Harris, *A Story of Carn Brea*)

ST ANTONY

Lord you are my island, in your bosom I rest
You are the calm of the sea, in that peace I lie
You are the deep waves of the ocean, in their depths I stay
You are the smooth white strand of the shore, in its swell I sing
You are the ocean of life that laps my being
In you is my eternal joy.

(Attributed to St Columba)

* * *

The bright field
I have seen the sun break through
to illuminate a small field
for a while, and gone my way
and forgotten it. But that was the pearl
of great price, the one field that had
the treasure in it. I realize now
that I must give all that I have
to possess it. Life is not hurrying

on to a receding future, nor hankering after
an imagined past. It is the turning
aside like Moses to the miracle
of the lit bush, to a brightness
that seemed as transitory as your youth
once, but is the eternity that awaits you.

(R.S. Thomas, *Laboratories of the Spirit*, 20th century)

47

the celtic heart

The Gothic window where I sit
  Looks out upon the moor,
And Autumn's hand has thickly strewn
  The dry leaves at our door.
But o'er the hills I dimly see
  Another golden morn,
My father led me by the hand
  Through fields of waving corn.

(John Harris, *My Autobiography*)

* * *

A robin-redbreast singing in a storm
On the fence-top of a sudden burst of song
  Fell strangely on my ear,
From robin-redbreast the bare boughs among,
  Who warbled full and clear.

The minstrel of the storm was hidden there
  Within a blasted tree.
When adverse tempest strip hope's branches bare,
  O may I sing like thee.

(John Harris)

ST ANTONY

I lie on my back
amid the sweet grasses
waving in the warm wind
and watch the lark rising
in the clear blue of the sky
above.
Harebells nod in the breeze
and the waves
roar, hurling themselves
on the rocks below.
The lark trills its sweet song
As the white sea birds
wheel and turn about my head.
I sigh
and my dear, sweet Lord is by my side.
Was there ever such a place
where heaven touched earth
as this?

(*Gormola Kernewek*)

6

ST MARTIN

ST Martin was born in Hungary and enlisted in the Roman army as an officer. In the winter of AD 337 when the army was serving in Amiens in France, a semi-naked beggar approached him one day, shivering with cold. Much to the amusement of his fellow officers, Martin sliced his red officer's cloak in half and gave half to the beggar. That night in a dream he saw Christ, dressed in the half-cloak and talking to the disciples. 'See,' He was saying, 'see what a fine cloak Martin gave me today!'

Martin obtained a discharge from the army and was baptized. In AD 360 he joined Bishop Hilary at Poitiers and founded the monastery at Liguge, the first in Gaul. Martin was much influenced by the lives of the desert saints such as Antony and Paul the Hermit and longed for the opportunity to live in isolation himself. But he was a charismatic figure and a born leader and the Church, recognizing his gifts, appointed him Bishop of Tours in AD 372. As an ex-soldier used to obeying orders Martin submitted to the will of the Church, but his teaching about living a simple life and finding a desert place in a world of increasing wealth and secularization came as a breath of fresh air. Young men and women were drawn to his dynamic preaching. Influenced by the lives of the desert Fathers, inspired by the Gospel of St John and steeped in their love of the Psalms, these young Christians left Tours each in search of their own 'desert' place. Martin had launched the beginnings of a spiritual revolution.

St Martin died in AD 397 and the story of his life was written by his friend Sulpicius Severus. It was full of miracle stories and quickly became a best-seller and a model for future 'lives' of saints.

Martin's feast day is on 11 November.

Christ in friend and stranger

You are the caller
You are the poor
You are the stranger at my door

The Celtic Heart

You are the wanderer
The unfed
You are the homeless
With no bed

You are the man
Driven insane
You are the child
Crying in pain

You are the other who comes to me
If I open to another you're born in me.
(David Adam, *The Edge of Glory*)

* * *

Rune of hospitality
I saw a stranger yestreen;
I put food in the eating place,
Drink in the drinking place,
Music in the listening place;
And, in the sacred name of the Triune,
He blessed myself and my house,
My cattle and my dear ones.
And the lark said in her song,
    Often, often, often,
Goes the Christ in the stranger's guise:

ST MARTIN

Often, often, often,
Goes the Christ in the stranger's guise.

(Traditional Irish)

* * *

Whether the sun is at its height, or the moon and stars pierce the darkness, my little hut is always open. It shall never be closed to anyone, lest I should close it to Christ himself.

Whether my guest is rich and noble, or whether he is poor and ragged, my tiny larder is always open. I shall never refuse to share my food, lest the Son of Mary should go hungry.

(Traditional)

* * *

I see my Lord in your sad eyes
I see Him on His knees
'O let this cup be gone from me'
I hear His frightened pleas.

With all my failings, all my faults,
Your helpmeet I would be.
If I see Christ in you my friend
Can you see Him in me?

(*Gormola Kernewek*)

When Jesus commands us to love our neighbours, he does not only mean our human neighbours; he means all the animals and birds, insects and plants, amongst whom we live. Just as we should not be cruel to other human beings, so we should not be cruel to any species of creature. Just as we should love and cherish other human beings, so we should love and cherish all God's creation.

We learn to love other human beings by discerning their pleasure and pain, their joy and sorrow, and by sympathizing with them. We need only poke a horse with a sharp stick to discern the pain it can suffer; and when we stroke and slap that same horse on the neck, we can feel its pleasure. Thus we can love a horse in the same way we can love another human being. Of course, our love for other species is less full and less intense than our love for humans, because the range and depth of their feelings are less than our own. Yet we should remember that all love comes from God, so when our love is directed towards an animal or even a tree, we are participating in the fullness of God's love.

(Pelagius, 'To an elderly friend', from *Letters of Pelagius*, trans. Robert Van de Weyer, 4th/5th century)

ST MARTIN

I should welcome the poor to my feast,
For they are God's children.
I should welcome the sick to my feast,
For they are God's joy.
Let the poor sit with Jesus at the highest place,
And the sick dance with the angels.

God bless the poor,
God bless the sick;
And bless our human race.

God bless our food,
God bless our drink,
All homes, O God, embrace.

(Traditional)

* * *

There is no point in abstaining from bodily food if you do not have love in your heart. Those who do not fast much but who take great care to keep their heart pure (on which, as they know, their life ultimately depends) are better off than those who are vegetarian, or travel in carriages, and think they are therefore superior to everyone else. To these people death has entered through the window of their pride.

(Gildas, 6th century)

The Celtic Heart

Bless, O Lord, the food we eat
and if there be any poor creature
hungry or thirsty walking along the road
send them into us that we can share the food with them
just as you share your gifts with all of us.

Remember the poor when you look out on fields you own,
on your plump cows grazing.

Remember the poor when you look into your barn, at the
abundance of your harvest.

Remember the poor when the wind howls and the rain falls,
as you sit warm and dry in your house.

Remember the poor when you eat fine meat and drink fine
ale, at your fine carved table.

The cows have grass to eat, the rabbits have burrows for
shelter, the birds have warm nests.

But the poor have no food except what you feed them,
no shelter except your house when you welcome them,
no warmth except your glowing fire.

(Traditional Celtic, 8th century)

ST MARTIN

When you sit happy in your own fair house,
Remember all poor men that are abroad,
That Christ, who gave this roof, prepare for thee
Eternal dwelling in the house of God.

(Alcuin of York, 8th century)

* * *

Christ has no body on earth but yours
No hands but yours
No feet but yours
Yours are the eyes through which Christ's compassion
    is to look out for the world
Yours are the feet with which he is to go about doing good
Yours are the hands with which he is to bless us now.

(Teresa of Avila, 16th century)

τbe ceλτιc bearτ

I thought Love lived in the hot sunshine,
But O he lives in the moony light!
I thought to find Love in the heat of the day,
But sweet Love is the comforter of night.

Seek Love in the pity of other's woe,
In the gentle relief of another's care,
In the darkness of night and the winter's snow,
In the naked and outcast, seek Love there.

(William Blake, 18th/19th century)

* * *

I know perfectly well that poverty and misfortune suit me better than
riches and pleasure. Christ the Lord, himself, was poor for our sakes.

(St Patrick, 5th century)

7

PELAGIUS

PELAGIUS was the Latin name of the Celtic–British theologian Morgan who by AD 380 was making a name for himself in Rome. Pelagius was a knowledgeable and well-respected teacher, and when he attacked St Augustine's treatise on predestination and original sin he gained a considerable following in Rome. Pelagius' thoughts on the matter were accepted by most Celtic–British Christians of the time.

He held that newborn children are as innocent as Adam was when he was first created, and that men and women are created good and are given by God the will to do good or evil as they choose. He also held that the whole human race does not die because of Adam's death or sin, and neither will everyone rise again because of Christ's resurrection. He believed that good works are important and that even before the coming of Christ there had been people wholly without sin.

Pelagius left Rome before the Goths sacked the city in AD 410 and made his way to Carthage. In Carthage Augustine had many followers and Pelagius soon found himself embroiled in bitter arguments. His condemnation of a society in which he believed there was one law for the rich and another for the poor made him more unpopular still. In AD 417 Pope Innocent I declared Pelagius' teaching to be heretical and ordered his excommunication. Pelagius retired to the Holy Land where, although attacked by Jerome, he was supported and protected by John, Bishop of Jerusalem. He died in Palestine in the 430s.

His views were shared by most of the Celtic Christians of Gaul and Britain, so when he died the beliefs that had become known as Pelagianism lived on, even though the Church authorities and councils condemned them as heretical. So strongly were the beliefs held in Britain that in AD 429 Germanus, Bishop of Auxerre, was sent to stamp them out. He was unsuccessful and went again on the same mission in AD 440. Even now, the old Celtic hatred of the concept of original sin and predestination lingers on in fiercely independent British hearts.

The mind of Christ

Think of Him going on His way alone, past the home where the wearied labourers sat amidst the happy family and blessed God for the simple evening repast. Think of Him as the sun sank behind the western hills, and the bud flew to its shelter within the nest, and the fox crept to its home beneath the rocks. Stillness lay on the villages where the households slept in happy safety. But He went through the night weary, homeless, hungry, cold. The Son of Man had nowhere to lay His head.

(Mark Guy Pearse, *Some Aspects of a Blessed Life*, 19th century)

* * *

Thou art God
Thou art the peace of all things calm
Thou art the place to hide from harm
Thou art the light that shines in dark
Thou art the heart's eternal spark
Thou art the door that's open wide
Thou art the guest who waits inside
Thou art the stranger at the door
Thou art the calling of the poor
Thou art my Lord and with me still
Thou art my love, keep me from ill
Thou art the light, the truth, the way
Thou art my Saviour this very day

(David Adam, *The Edge of Glory*)

The Celtic Heart

Deus meus adiuva me,
Give me Thy love, O Christ, I pray,
Give me Thy love, O Christ, I pray,
Deus meus adiuva me.

In meum cor ut sanum sit,
Pour, loving King, Thy love in it,
Pour, loving King, Thy love in it,
In meum cor ut sanum sit.

Domine, da ut peto a te,
O, pure bright sun, give, give today,
O, pure bright sun, give, give today,
Domine, da ut peto a te.

Hanc spero rem et quaero quam
Thy love to have where'er I am,
Thy love to have where'er I am,
Hanc spero rem et quaero quam.

Tuum amorem sicut vis,
Give to me swiftly, strongly, this,
Give to me swiftly, strongly, this,
Tuum amorem sicut vis.

pelagius

Domine, Domine, exaudi me,
Fill my soul, Lord, with Thy love's ray,
Fill my soul, Lord, with Thy love's ray,
Domine, Domine, exaudi me.

Deus meus adiuva me,
Deus meus adiuva me.

(Translated by George Sigerson, from
Bards of the Gael and Gall, 18th century)

* * *

A bud, a flower, a little child – these are the voices that speak to men of
God; all that is glad, all this is beautiful, all that is trustful and loving,
all that tells of tenderness and constant care – these are Christ's chosen
emblems of the Most High.

(Mark Guy Pearse, *Come Break Your Fast*)

* * *

Dear, chaste Christ,
Who can see into every heart and read every mind,
Take hold of my thoughts.
Bring my thoughts back to me
And clasp me to yourself.

(Prayer of a Celtic monk, 8th century)

ᴛʜe cᴇʟᴛɪc ʜeᴀʀᴛ

Lord, who made sea and land
always give me aid,
And guide my life here
in the way of truth.
Lord Jesu, look on me
and grant me thy unfailing grace.
Every hour, Jesu, it is my desire
In this world to please you.

(Prayer of St Meryadoc,
from *Beunans Meriasek,* 2538, 14th century)

* * *

Jesus, Lord of heaven and earth
And Saviour to us likewise,
Forgive me my trespass,
for great is my remorse:

I have, indeed, keen repentance
For denying Thee, now:
I beseech mercy at all times
Certainly from a full heart.

(Peter, 'Resurrexio Domini',
Cornish Ordinalia, 14th century)

peLAGIUS

O Jesus, Son of God, who wast silent before Pilate, do not let us wag our tongues without thinking of what we are to say and how to say it.
(Irish–Gaelic prayer)

* * *

Lord of my heart
Give me vision to inspire me
That, working or resting,
I may always think of you.

Lord of my heart
Give me light to guide me
That, at home or abroad,
I may always walk in your way.

Lord of my heart
Give me wisdom to direct me
That, thinking or acting,
I may always discern right from wrong.

Heart of my own heart
Whatever befall me
Rule over my thoughts and feelings
My words and actions.

(Ancient Irish)

Come to me, Lord,
In the refreshing, strengthening, heart-warming, soul-rejoicing manifestations of thy presence: for thy love is better than wine, and the very crumb from under thy table is more delicious than the honey and the honey-comb.

(Robert Hawker DD, 19th century)

* * *

Blessed, holy, compassionate Lord God! For Jesus' sake fulfil this promise daily in my soul: bear me up, carry me through, and strengthen me in the Lord my God, that I may indeed walk up and down in his name until thou bring me in to see his face in thine eternal home, and dwell under the light of his countenance for ever.

(Robert Hawker)

* * *

My soul, ponder these things. Hath the Lord lighted thy candle? Is Jesus thy light, thy life, thy joy, thy sunshine, thy morning star, thy all in all? And hath he risen upon thee, never more to go down? O, then, though all thou knowest, all thou beholdest now, is but as the faint taper of the night, compared to the glory of that day which shall be revealed. Yet take to thyself by faith all the sweet comforts of thy state of grace, and say, it is the Lord that hath lighted my candle.

(Robert Hawker)

pelagius

Come with me and share my vision,
See before us countryside,
Green the fields,
Gentle rising hill with trees far off,
See as though within the depth of
your mind's eye;
Feel that wind, warm yet gentle,
The sun is touching on your hair.
Nearby the stream,
Ripple water over stones
and make a mirrored pool,
Wherein reflects the heaven:
A canopy of sky so blue,
Yet dappled neatly with the edging cloud
of white,
So like a gossamered cocoon of light,
You feel that should your being touch it,
Just like the gentle snowflake would it disappear:
A bird is singing songs you think you've
never heard before, but have,
And in the air the fragrance of a hundred
flowers is smelt,
So delicately confused are they,
You cannot tell the other from the one.

the celtic heart

We wait and watch,
The day is quiet, save for the sounds described,
Our bodies rest, our minds unfold,
And into this peaceful solitude release
you soul,
Let now the conscience be your sleepy guide,
Relax, unwind, drink in the beauty shown,
And thank the Giver.

(Paul Randall-Morris, *Poems from the Heart*, 20th century)

8

ST JEROME

ST Jerome was born of Christian parents at Strido near Aquitea around AD 342. As a young man Jerome studied rhetoric in Rome for eight years. He then travelled in Gaul before returning to Aquitea and setting up a community of ascetics with his friends. The community survived for only three years and in AD 374 he set out for Syria. He settled as a hermit at Chalcis in the Syrian desert for nearly five years in order to learn Hebrew. He was ordained priest in Antioch and in AD 382 returned to Rome, where he was appointed secretary to Pope Damusus. Damusus commissioned Jerome to revise the Latin version of the Psalms and New Testament. Eventually Jerome translated the whole of the Bible into the Latin version which is today known as the Vulgate. When Damusus died, Jerome visited Antioch, Egypt and Palestine, and in AD 386 he finally settled in Bethlehem. He was accompanied by two women friends from Rome, Paula and Eustachium, and for the rest of his life he devoted himself to his studies, writing letters to Christian friends and establishing a monastery. He also founded a hospice for pilgrims. Paula and Eustachium set about founding a convent.

Busy though he was, Jerome made retreats in one of the many caves close to the spot where Jesus was born. Towards the end of his life he rarely left the cave and allowed himself to become the ascetic he had longed to be all his life.

Jerome was a passionate man who threw himself into controversies. He championed the Celtic followers of Martin of Tours in their struggle to live a solitary life in the wilds of western Britain, often writing letters of encouragement, but he was quick to condemn Celtic support for Pelagianism and bitterly attacked Pelagius and his beliefs. He died in Bethlehem in AD 420.

Jerome's feast day is on 30 September.

Steadfastness of faith

He is a bird round which a trap is closed
A leaking ship unfit for a wild sea
An empty vessel and a withered tree –
Who lays aside God's wishes unimposed.

He is the sun's bright rays, pure gold and fine,
A silver chalice overfilled with wine
Holy and happy, beautiful in love –
Who does the will of God in heaven above.

(An Irish lyric, *c.* 8th century)

* * *

In name of Father,
In name of Son,
In name of Spirit,
    Three in One:

Father cherish me,
Son cherish me,
Spirit cherish me,
    Three all-kindly.

God make me holy,
Christ make me holy,
Spirit make me holy,
    Three all-holy.

the celtic heart

Three aid my hope,
Three aid my love,
Three aid mine eye,
 And my knee from stumbling,
 My knee from stumbling.

(Carmina Gadelica, III, 63)

* * *

Now there are three kinds of martyrdom which are counted as a cross to man, that is to say, white martyrdom, and green martyrdom, and red martyrdom.

This is the white martyrdom to man, when he separates for the sake of God from everything he loves, although he suffer fasting or labour thereat.

This is the green martyrdom to him, when by means of them (fasting and penance) he separates from his desires, or suffers toil in penance and repentance.

This is the red martyrdom to him, endurance of a cross or destruction for Christ's sake, as has happened to the apostles in the persecution of the wicked and in teaching the law of God.

These three kinds of martyrdom are comprised in the carnal ones who resort to good repentance, who separate from their desires, who pour forth their blood in fasting and in labour for Christ's sake.

(Whitley Stokes and John Strachan,
Thesaurus Palaeo-Libernicus Voii, Dublin, 20th century)

ST JEROME

Eternal light shine in our hearts
Eternal goodness deliver us from evil
Eternal power be our support
Eternal wisdom scatter the darkness
of our ignorance.

Eternal pity have mercy on us
That with all our heart and mind
and soul and strength we may seek thy face
and be brought by thine infinite mercy
to thy holy presence.

(Alcuin of York)

* * *

Jesus, Lord, full of grace
    Worship to thee and joy
Jesu, Lord in every place,
    Keep my soul without corruption,
    And my body likewise.
Blessed Mary, pure virgin,
Mary be my succour,
Mary, whom I love much,
    To dear God pray on my behalf.

(*Beunans Meriasek*, 3860)

The Celtic Heart

High on the wild moor
Where no trees grow
And Heaven leans low
to kiss the earth.

Grey rocks, worn
by the footsteps of
angels,
Stand sentinel.

And God steps down
to walk on earth.

O that my heart
was as steadfast
and sure
as those granite boulders
fashioned by eternity.

In my frailty and my fear
all I have are
my longings.
Are they enough
to become a stairway
for your love?

(*Gormola Kernewek*)

ST JEROME

As it was,
As it is,
As it shall be
Evermore,
O Thou Triune
Of grace!
With the ebb,
With the flow,
O Thou Triune
Of grace!
With the ebb,
With the flow.
(*Carmina Gadelica*, II, 217)

* * *

Father God, your love surrounds us,
Cove and headland, sea and sand
Sing the praises of your beauty,
Show the hallmark of your hand.
Give us eyes to see your glory,
Ear attentive, hearts aflame,
Voices raised in nature's anthem
To the worship of your name.

The Celtic Heart

God in Christ, your grace surrounds us,
Balm in sadness, hope in pain,
Costly love that seeks and finds us,
Bears us gently home again.
Grant to us, your pilgrim people,
Joy to serve and strength to lead,
Grace to share and live your message,
Gospel word and gospel deed.

Spirit God, your power surrounds us,
Power of tempest, wind and wave,
Source of sainthood, artist's vision,
Life that conquers sin and grave.
Pour your sevenfold gifts upon us
Minds to open, hearts to move.
Gather in the whole creation
To the banquet of your love.

(Perran Gay, 20th century)

9

ST JOHN CHRYSOSTOM

ST John was born in Antioch around AD 347 to a Christian mother and a pagan father. Antioch was one of the most beautiful and cosmopolitan cities of the eastern Mediterranean and John's childhood was comfortable and happy. He was educated by tutors until he was 14, when he went to university. Taught by the great teacher Libanus, John soon drew attention to himself with the quickness of his mind and his ability to express himself. He could have made a career in the world of education, but when he was 18 John encountered the monk Diodorus who lived as a hermit in the mountains. He became strongly attracted to the ascetic life. He was baptized and joined a community where for a year he practised asceticism in a moderate manner. Later he decided to go further in terms of self-mortification. He retired to a cave, denied himself sleep, read the Bible continually and spent two years without lying down. The result was inevitable. His stomach shrivelled up, his kidneys were damaged by cold and his digestion became permanently impaired. His health ruined, John had learned his lesson. He returned to Antioch and although he always admired the lives of the hermits, he set himself against a life of such self-mortification.

In AD 386 John was appointed presbyter with a special responsibility for preaching. His sermons and writings were inspired and his ability earned him the name Chrysostom (golden tongue). In AD 398 he was made Patriarch of Constantinople and he immediately set about the work of reforming the city, the courts and the Church. In the process he made many enemies, especially Theophilus, the Patriarch of Alexandria, and the Empress Theodosia. In AD 403 his enemies conspired to bring charges against him and John was removed from his see.

In AD 404 he was sent into exile. His first exile was near his home in Antioch, but when it became obvious that, although ill, he was not going to die and was attracting too many followers, he was forced to march in severe weather to Aribassus, some 60 miles to the north. After he had spent a year there, orders came for him to be moved yet again. He was suffering from a fever even before he left and the rain fell continuously. Three months later, on 14 September 407, he died by the roadside in Comana. There were many tributes to him after his death, but the best was spoken by his pupil Cassian of Marseilles: 'It would be a great thing to attain to his stature, but it would be hard. Nevertheless even the following of him is lovely and magnificent.'

John Chrysostom's feast day is on 27 January.

The wonder of God's creation

Look at the sky, how beautiful it is, and how vast, all crowned with a blazing diadem of stars! For how many ages has it existed? Already it has been there for five thousand years, and shows no signs of ageing. Like some young creature full of sap it preserves all the shining and the freshness of an earlier age, and manifests the beauty it possessed in the beginning, and time has not wearied it. And this vast, beautiful, ageless sky, unchangeable and gleaming, with all its stars, having existed through so many ages – this same God, who some profess to be able to see with mortal eyes and comprehend with their own pitiable intelligence – this same God created it as easily as a man, throwing a handful of sticks together, creates a hut. And this is what Isaiah meant when he said, 'He stretches out the heavens as a curtain, and spreadeth them out as a tent to dwell in.'

Look at the great mass of the mountains, and all the innumerable people who dwell on earth, and the plants, all so rich and wonderfully varied, and the towns and the vast buildings and the wild animals, and all these the earth supports easily on her back. And yet with all its vastness, it was fashioned by God 'as though it were nothing'. So speaks for us Isaiah, searching for a phrase which will explain the ease with which God created the earth ... And then look at the inhabitants of earth, of whom the prophet said, 'He sitteth upon the circle of the earth, and the inhabitants thereof are as grasshoppers,' and a little while earlier he said, 'Behold the nations are as a drop of water falling from a bowl.' Think of all the peoples who inhabit the earth: Syrians, Cilicians, Cappadocians, Bithynians, those who live on the shores of the Black Sea, in Thrace, in Macedonia, in all of Greece and the islands of Britain, Sarmatia, India and the inhabitants of Persia, and then of all the innumerable other peoples and races, and all these are 'as a drop of water falling from a bowl'. And what small atom of this drop of water thinks he can know God?

(St John Chrysostom, *De Incomprehensibili*, II, 6, 4th century)

* * *

Understand, if you want to know the Creator, created things.

(Columbanus, 7th century)

* * *

O, King of the Tree of Life
The blossoms on the branches are your people
The singing birds are your angels
The whispering breeze is your Spirit

O, King of the Tree of Life
May the blossoms bring forth the sweetest fruit
May the birds sing out the highest praise
May your Spirit cover all with gentle breath.

(Traditional)

ST JOHN CHRYSOSTOM

I see his blood upon the rose
And in the stars the glory of his eyes
His body gleams amid eternal snows
His tears fall from the skies.

I see his face in every flower
The thunder and the singing of the birds
Are but his voice – and carven by his power
Rocks are written words.

All pathways by his feet are worn
His strong heart stirs the ever beating sea
His crown of thorns is twined with every thorn
His cross is every tree.

(Joseph Mary Plunkett, Ireland, 20th century)

* * *

Earth teach me stillness as the grasses are stilled with light
Earth teach me suffering as old stones suffer with memory
Earth teach me humility as blossoms are humble with beginning
Earth teach me caring as the mother who secures her young
Earth teach me courage as the tree which stands all alone
Earth teach me limitation as the ant which crawls on the ground
Earth teach me freedom as the eagle which soars in the sky
Earth teach me resignation as the leaves which die in the fall
Earth teach me to forget myself as melted snow forgets its life

Earth teach me to remember kindness as dry fields weep for rain.
(Ute Prayer)

* * *

Look at the animals roaming the forest: God's spirit dwells within them. Look at the birds flying across the sky: God's spirit dwells within them. Look at the tiny insects crawling upon the grass: God's spirit dwells within them. Look at the fish in the river and sea: God's spirit dwells within them. There is no creature on earth in whom God is absent. Travel across the ocean to the most distant land, and you will find God's spirit in all the creatures there. Climb up the highest mountain, and you will find God's spirit among the creatures who live at the summit. When God pronounced that his creation was good, it was not only that his hand had fashioned every creature; it was that his breath had brought every creature to life.

Look, too, at the great trees of the forest; look at the wild flowers and the grass in the field; look even at your crops. God's spirit is present within all plants as well. The presence of God's spirit in all living beings is what makes them beautiful; and if we look with God's eyes, nothing on the earth is ugly.

(Pelagius, 'To an elderly friend', *Letters of Pelagius*, trans. R. Van de Weyer)

ST JOHN CHRYSOSTOM

Creation of the world

My dear King, my own King, without pride, without sin,
you created the whole world, eternal, victorious King.

King above the elements, King above the sun, King beneath
the ocean, King of the north and south, the east and west,
against you no enemy can prevail.

King of the Mysteries, you existed before the elements,
before the sun was set in the sky, before the waters covered
the ocean floor; beautiful King, you are without beginning
and without end.

King, you created the daylight, and made the darkness; you
are not arrogant or boastful, and yet strong and firm.

King, you created the land out of shapeless mass, you carved the
mountains and chiselled the valleys, and covered the earth with trees
and grass.

King, you stretched out the sky above the earth, a perfect sphere like a
perfect apple, and you decorated the sky with stars to shine at night.

King, you pierced the earth with springs from which pure water flows,
to form streams and rivers across the land.

King, you ordained the eight winds, the four primary winds from north and south, east and west, and the four lesser winds that swirl hither and thither.

You gave each wind its own colour: the north wind is white, bringing snow in winter; the south wind is red, carrying warmth in summer; the west wind is blue, a cooling breeze across the sea; the east wind is yellow, scorching in summer and bitter in winter; and the lesser winds are green, orange, purple and black – the black wind that blows in the darkest nights.

King, you measured each object and each span within the universe: the heights of the mountains and the depths of the oceans; the distance from the sun to the moon, and from star to star.

You ordained the movements of every object: the sun to cross the sky each day, and the moon to rise each night; the clouds to carry rain from the sea, and the rivers to carry water back from the sea.

King, you divided the earth into three zones: the north cold and bitter; the south hot and dry: and the middle zone cool, wet and fertile.

And you created men and women to be your stewards of the earth, always praising you for your boundless love.

ST JOHN CHRYSOSTOM

Creation of heaven

King, you created heaven according to your delight, a place that is safe and pure, its air filled with the songs of angels.

It is like a strong mighty city, which no enemy can invade, with walls as high as mountains.

It is like an open meadow, in which all can move freely, with people arriving from earth but never leaving.

It is huge, ten times the size of earth, so that every creature ever born can find a place.

It is small, no bigger than a village, where all are friends, and none is a stranger.

In the centre is a palace, its walls made of emerald and its gates of amethyst; and on each gate is hung a golden cross.

The roof is ruby, and at each pinnacle stands an eagle covered in gold, its eyes of sapphire.

Inside the palace it is always daylight, and the air cool, nether hot nor cold; and there is a perfect green lawn, with a blue stream running across it.

At the edge of this lawn are trees and shrubs, always in blossom, white, pink and purple, spreading a sweet fragrance everywhere.

Round the lawn walks a King, not dressed in fine robes, but in a simple white tunic, smiling, and embracing those he meets.

And people from outside are constantly entering the palace, mingling one with another, and then leaving.

Everyone in heaven is free to come to the palace, and then to take with them its perfect peaceful joy; and in this way the whole of heaven is infused with the joy of the palace.

(*The Celtic Psalter*,
attributed to Oengus the Culdee,
Ireland, 9th century)

* * *

The firmament was covered with stars … How brightly they beamed in their mystic orbits in the blue deeps of ether. The universe looked like a bright palace of gems, where angels banqueted at the table of love … Suddenly my father in a soft and solemn voice, befitting the majesty of the moment, exclaimed, 'God is author of all this, my son. He has made the stars also.'

(John Harris, *My Autobiography*)

ST JOHN CHRYSOSTOM

O Son of God, change my heart.

Your spirit composes the songs of the birds and the buzz of the bees.

Your creation is a million wondrous miracles, beautiful to look upon,

I ask of you just one more miracle:

beautify my soul.

(Traditional)

10

ST DAVID

The story of St David's life was written by Bishop Rhygyfarch during the tenth century. According to this history, David's father was Sant, a former king of Ceredigion (the old name for Cardigan in Wales) who had abdicated to take up the religious life; his mother was Non, a student at the monastery of Ty Gwyn whose father was of noble birth. His conception was the result of a very short relationship and after Sant had left the area, Non was made to leave the monastery. She gave birth to a stillborn baby boy in a small hut near the standing stones beyond Bryn y Garn during a violent thunderstorm. Present at the birth was St Ailbe, who took the child, resuscitated him and baptized him in the nearby spring. St Ailbe took charge of the baby and Non went to Cornwall, where she founded the Church of Altarnon.

David grew up in the monastery at Yr Henllwyn and from there he went as a student to Illtyd's monastery at Llantwit Major.

David was a gentle man who was loved by all who knew him. Bishop Rhygyfarch tells us, 'He spent all day, never turning from his task nor wearying, in teaching and kneeling in prayer and caring for the brethren; also he fed innumerable orphans, waifs, widows, the poor, the sick, the weak and pilgrims.' He became the founder of 12 monasteries and travelled all over Wales and south-western England. He finally settled at Mynyw, where he established an abbey. His monks led a life of extreme asceticism modelled on that of the Eastern Fathers, particularly on the life of St Antony. The abbey at Mynyw was built on the site of the present-day St David's Cathedral. David died in AD 601 and was accepted as the patron saint of Wales during the twelfth century.

David's feast day is on 1 March.

God and the soul

Mark the sea-bird wildly wheeling
Through the storm skies;
God defends him, God attends him,
When he cries.

(Mark Guy Pearse, *Come Break Your Fast*)

Τhe Celτic heart

God

I am the wind that breathes upon the sea,
I am the wave on the ocean,
I am the murmur of leaves rustling,
I am the rays of the sun,
I am the beam of the moon and stars,
I am the power of trees growing,
I am the bud breaking into blossom,
I am the movement of the salmon swimming,
I am the courage of the wild boar fighting,
I am the speed of the stag running,
I am the strength of the ox pulling the plough,
I am the size of the mighty oak tree,
And I am the thoughts of all people
Who praise my beauty and grace.

The soul

I am a flame of fire, blazing with passionate love;
I am a spark of light, illuminating the deepest truth;
I am a rough ocean, heaving with righteous anger;
I am a calm lake, comforting the troubled breast;
I am a wild storm, raging at human sins;
I am a gentle breeze, blowing hope in the saddened heart;
I am dry dust, choking worldly ambition;

ST DAVID

I am wet earth, bearing rich fruits of grace.

(*The Black Book of Carmarthen*, 12th century)

* * *

By the singing of hymns eagerly ringing out
By thousands of angels rejoicing in holy dances
And by the four living creatures full of eyes
With the twenty-four joyful elders
Casting their crowns under the feet of the Lamb of God
The Trinity is praised in eternal threefold exchanges.

(*Altus Prosator*, attributed to St Columba)

* * *

To you, Creator of nature and humanity, of truth and beauty, I pray:

Hear my voice, for it is the voice of the victims of all wars and violence among individuals and nations.

Hear my voice, when I beg you to instil into the hearts of all human beings the wisdom of peace, the strength of justice and the joy of fellowship.

Hear my voice, for I speak for the multitudes in every country and in every period of history who do not want war and are ready to walk the road of peace.

(Pope John Paul II, 20th century)

tbe celtic beart

Three joints in the finger, but only one finger fair
Three leaves of the shamrock yet only one shamrock to wear
Frost, snowflakes and ice, yet all in water their origin share
Three Persons in God; to one God alone we make prayer.
(Traditional Irish)

* * *

Clear and high in the perfect assembly
Let us praise above the nine grades of angels
The sublime and blessed Trinity.

Purely, humbly, in skilful verse
I should love to give praise to the Trinity
According to the greatness of his power.

God has required of the host in this world
Who are his, that they should at all times
All together, fear the Trinity.
(Early Welsh)

* * *

St Ninian's catechism

Question What is best in this world?

Answer To do the will of our Maker.

Question What is his will?

Answer That we should live according to the laws of his creation.

Question How do we know those laws?

Answer   By study – studying the Scriptures with devotion.

Question What tool has our Maker provided for this study?

Answer   The intellect, which can probe everything.

Question And what is the fruit of study?

Answer   To perceive the eternal Word of God reflected in every plant and insect, every bird and animal, and every man and woman.

(St Ninian, 4th/5th century)

* * *

I would prepare a feast and be host to the great High King,
with all the company of heaven.
The sustenance of pure love be in my house,
the roots of repentance in my house.
Baskets of love be mine to give,
with cups of mercy for all the company.
Sweet Jesus, be there with us, with all the company of heaven.
May cheerfulness abound in the feast,
the feast of the great High King,
my host for all eternity.

(Traditional – sometimes attributed to Brigid of Kildare, 6th century)

the celtic heart

My God and my Chief,
  I seek to Thee in the morning,
My God and my Chief,
  I seek to Thee this night.
I am giving Thee my mind,
  I am giving Thee my will,
I am giving Thee my wish,
  My soul everlasting and my body.

Mayest Thou be chieftain over me,
  Mayest Thou be master unto me,
Mayest Thou be shepherd over me,
  Mayest Thou be guardian unto me,
Mayest Thou be herdsman over me,
  Mayest Thou be guide unto me,
Mayest Thou be with me, O Chief of chiefs,
  Father everlasting and God of the heavens.

(*Carmina Gadelica*, III, 347)

* * *

God be in my head, and in my understanding
God be in my eyes, and in my looking
God be in my mouth, and in my speaking;
God be in my heart, and in my thinking
God be at my end, and at my departing.

(*Old Sarum Primer*, 13th century)

ST DAVID

God to enfold me,
   God to surround me,
God in my speaking,
   God in my thinking.

God in my sleeping,
   God in my waking,
God in my watching,
   God in my hoping.

God in my life,
   God in my lips,
God in my soul,
   God in my heart.

(*Carmina Gadelica*, III, 53)

* * *

In the Father's name,
And in the Son's name,
In the Spirit's name,
   Three the same, One in name;

Father be my friend,
And Son be my friend,
Spirit be my friend,
   Three to send and befriend.

ᴛһᴇ ᴄᴇʟᴛɪᴄ һᴇᴀʀᴛ

God my holiness,
Christ my holiness,
Spirit holiness,
    Three to bless, holiness.

    Help of hope the Three,
    Help of love the Three,
    Help of sight the Three,
And my knee stumbling free,
From my knee stumbling free.

(G.R.D. McLean, *Praying with Highland Christians*)

* * *

Be thou my vision, O Lord of my heart,
Be all else but naught to me, save that thou art;
Be thou my best thought in the day and the night,
Both waking and sleeping, thy presence my light.
Be thou my wisdom, be thou my true word,
Be thou ever with me, and I with thee, Lord;
Be thou my great Father, and I thy true son;
Be thou in me dwelling, and I with thee one.
Be thou my breastplate, my sword for the fight;
Be thou my whole armour, be thou my true might;
Be thou my soul's shelter, be thou my strong tower;
O raise thou me heavenward, great power of my power.

ST DAVID

Riches I heed not, nor man's empty praise;
Be thou mine inheritance now and always;
Be thou and thou only the first in my heart;
O sovereign of heaven, my treasure thou art.
High king of heaven, thou heaven's bright sun
O grant me its joys after vict'ry is won;
Great heart of my own heart, whatever befall,
Still be thou my vision, O ruler of all.

(Celtic prayer, translated by Mary Byrne,
versified by Eleanor Hull, 18th/19th century)

* * *

Lord Jesu, help me:
I cannot help myself.
   Blinded am I by whiteness.
I know not, by my charity
What is the radiance
   That is around me, all around me.

(*Beunans Meriasek*, 3665)

The Celtic Heart

Good to me it is
To draw near to God.
   And to worship Him,
To do His will,
As behoveth,
   So that I may earn heaven's kingdom.

(*Beunans Meriasek*, 1098)

11

ST PATRICK

ST Patrick was the son of a Romano-British deacon named Calpurnius and the grandson of a priest called Potitus. He was born in AD 389 in the village of Bannavem, thought to be in northern England near Carlisle. At the age of 16 he was captured by raiders and taken as a slave to Ireland. After six years he managed to escape and was reluctantly given a berth on board a boat carrying hunting dogs to Gaul. In Gaul Patrick entered the monastery at Lerins and in AD 416 he was ordained deacon at Auxerre by Bishop Amator. He never forgot his time in Ireland and when he was 42 years old he was given the opportunity to return, being sent to assist Palladius in his mission to stamp out Pelagianism in Ireland. When Palladius died the following year, St Germanus of Auxerre consecrated Patrick as Bishop of Ireland.

Patrick began his work of preaching and establishing churches in Leinster and Meath, and in his writings he frequently said that he expected to be enslaved again or violently killed. The rule of the Druids was all-powerful and Patrick was often afraid.

Armed with 'the breastplate of Christ', Patrick plucked up courage to go to the court of the High King Laoghaire at Tara in Meath (having been in hiding from him after the Beltane fire incident described in Chapter 2). Here after much debate he wrung from the King a concession for Christianity to be preached and for Christians to be allowed to live in peace. He converted several members of the royal family. After visiting Rome in AD 442, he returned once more to Ireland and in AD 444 he founded the cathedral church of Armach, which was to become the educational and administrative centre of the Irish Church.

Christianity had arrived in Ireland before Patrick, but believers were isolated and scattered, particularly in the north, with small groups huddling together for protection against the power of the Druids. The religious tolerance which followed the meeting with High King Laoghaire meant that Patrick could gather these scattered groups together and bring them into a closer relationship with the rest of the Western Church. He tried hard to encourage the study of Latin and raise the general standards of scholarship.

During his mission in Ireland, he ordained over 300 bishops and 3,000 presbyters, and legend tells us that, after successfully wringing concessions for all Christians from High King Laoghaire, Patrick began a great debate with Jesus himself, from whom he eventually obtained special concessions for the Irish people. He asked that even if their repentance was on their deathbeds, the Irish should be allowed entrance to heaven, and that he and not St Peter would be at the gate to judge them. He prayed that the pagans would never overcome him and that no Irish person should be left alive to suffer the reign of the Antichrist. He also begged that Ireland would sink beneath the waves seven years before the day of doom.

Patrick's allegiance to the Roman Western Church meant that he was often at odds with the Celtic–British Christians, but such was his charisma and genuine devotion to the Irish people that he was held in great affection by all. He was well worthy to be called patron saint of Ireland.

Patrick's feast day is on 17 March.

Surrounded by God's protection

Circle me Lord
Keep protection near
And danger afar

Circle me Lord
Keep hope within

tbe celtic beart

Keep doubt without
Circle me Lord
Keep light near
And darkness afar

Circle me Lord
Keep peace within
Keep evil out.

(David Adam, *The Edge of Glory*)

* * *

The circle of Jesus keep you from sorrow
The circle of Jesus today and tomorrow
The circle of Jesus your foes confound
The circle of Jesus your life surround.

(David Adam, *The Edge of Glory*)

* * *

Toil together, struggle together, run together, suffer together, sleep together and rise together; as the servants, and assistants, and the ministers of God. Please him under whom you fight, and from whom you receive your wages. Let none of you be found a deserter. Let your baptism serve as a shield, your faith as a helmet, your love as a spear, your endurance as full armour. So be patient with one another in gentleness, as God is with you. Let me have joy of you always.

(St Ignatius, last letter to Polycarp, Bishop of Smyrna, *Ad Polycarpum VI*, 1st century)

Dear God, be good to me
The sea is so wide
And my boat is so small.

(Traditional Breton fisherman's prayer)

* * *

God created all human beings in God's image, to be like God. God has made animals more powerful than human beings, but we have been given intelligence and freedom.

We alone are able to recognize God as our maker, and therefore to understand the goodness of God's creation. We alone have the capacity to distinguish between good and evil, right and wrong. This means that our actions need not be compulsions, we do not have to be swayed by our immediate wants and desires, as are the animals. Instead, we can make choices. Day by day, hour by hour, we have to make decisions. In each decision we can choose either good or evil. This freedom to choose makes us like God. If we choose evil, that freedom becomes a curse. If we choose good, it becomes our greatest blessing.

(Pelagius, *Letters of Pelagius*, trans. R. Van de Weyer)

* * *

I rise up clothed in the strength of Christ.
I shall not be imprisoned, I shall not be harmed
I shall not be down-trodden, I shall not be left alone
I shall not be tainted, I shall not be overwhelmed

the celtic heart

I go clothed in Christ's white garments
I go freed to weave Christ's patterns
I go loved to serve Christ's weak ones
I go armed to rout out Christ's foes.

(A Celtic Eucharist,
Community of Aidan and Hilda)

* * *

Go on your way trusting in God and making the demons look silly.
(St Antony, 3rd/4th century)

* * *

Thou angel of God who hast charge of me
From the dear Father of mercifulness,
The shepherding kind of the fold of the saints
To make round about me this night;

Drive from me every temptation and danger,
Surround me on the sea of unrighteousness,
And in the narrows, crooks and straits,
Keep thou my coracle, keep it always.

Be thou a bright flame before me,
Be thou a guiding star above me,
Be thou a smooth path below me,
And be a kindly shepherd behind me,
Today, tonight, and for ever.

ST PATRICK

I am tired and I a stranger,
Lead thou me to the land of angels;
For me it is time to go home
To the court of Christ, to the peace of heaven.

(*Carmina Gadelica*, I, 49)

* * *

O Michael of the angels
And the righteous in heaven,
Shield thou my soul
  With the shade of thy wing;
Shield thou my soul
  On earth and in heaven;

From foes upon earth,
From foes beneath earth,
From foes in concealment
Protect and encircle
  My soul 'neath thy wing,
  Oh my soul with the shade of thy wing!

(*Carmina Gadelica*, III, 149)

The Three Who are over me,
The Three Who are below me,
The Three Who are above me here,
The Three Who are above me yonder;
The Three Who are in the earth,
The Three Who are in the air,
The Three Who are in the heaven,
The Three Who are in the great pouring sea.

(*Carmina Gadelica*, III, 93)

* * *

God with me lying down,
God with me rising up,
God with me in each ray of light,
Nor I a ray of joy without Him,
  Nor one ray without Him.

Christ with me sleeping,
Christ with me waking,
Christ with me watching,
Every day and night,
  Each day and night.

God with me protecting,
The Lord with me directing,
The Spirit with me strengthening,

ST PATRICK

For ever and for evermore,
    Ever and evermore, Amen.
    Chief of chiefs, Amen.

(*Carmina Gadelica*, I, 5)

            * * *

God to enfold,
God to surround,
God in speech-told,
God my thought-bound.

God when I sleep,
God when I wake,
God my watch-keep,
God my hope-sake.

God my life-whole,
God my lips apart,
God in my soul,
God in my heart.

God Wine and Bread,
God in my death,
God my soul-thread,
God ever breath.

(G.R.D. McLean, *Praying with Highland Christians*)

the celtic heart

The Three who are over my head,
The Three who are under my tread,
The Three who are over me here,
The Three who are over me there,
The Three who are in the earth near,
The Three who are up in the air,
The Three who in heaven do dwell,
The Three in the great ocean swell,
Pervading Three, O be with me.

(G.R.D. McLean, *Praying with Highland Christians*)

* * *

May the cross of Christ be over this face and this ear
May the cross of Christ be over this mouth and this throat
May the cross of Christ be over my arms
From my shoulder to my hands.

May the cross of Christ be with me, before me
May the cross of Christ be above me, behind me.

With the cross of Christ may I meet every
Difficulty in the heights and in the depths.
From the top of my head to the nail of my foot
I trust in the protection of your cross, O Christ.

(Attributed to Mugron, Abbot of Iona, 10th century)

A person might say that the world would be a better place if everyone within it were always good and never evil. But such a world would be flawed because it would lack one essential ingredient of goodness, namely freedom. When God created the world he was acting freely; no other force compelled God to create the world. Thus by creating humans in his image, God had to give them freedom. A person who could only do good and never do evil would be in chains; a person who can choose good or evil shares the freedom of God.

(Pelagius, *Letters to Pelagius*, trans. R. Van de Weyer)

* * *

I bind unto myself today
The strong name of the Trinity,
By invocation of the same,
The Three in One and One in Three.

I bind this day to me for ever,
By power of faith, Christ's Incarnation;
His baptism in the Jordan River;
His death on cross for my salvation;
His bursting from the spicèd tomb;
His riding up the heavenly way;
His coming at the day of doom;
I bind unto myself today.

THE CELTIC HEART

I bind unto myself the power
Of the great love of the Cherubim;
The sweet 'Well done' in judgement hour;
The service of the Seraphim,
Confessors' faith, Apostles' word,
The Patriarchs' prayers, the Prophets' scrolls.
All good deeds done unto the Lord,
And purity of virgin souls.

I bind unto myself today
The virtues of the starlit heaven,
The glorious sun's life-giving ray,
The whiteness of the moon at even,
The flashing of the lightning free,
The whirling wind's tempestuous shocks,
The stable earth, the deep salt sea,
Around the old eternal rocks.

I bind unto myself today
The power of God to hold and lead,
His eye to watch, His might to stay,
His ear to hearken to my need.
The wisdom of my God to teach,
His hand to guide, his shield to ward;

ST PATRICK

The word of God to give me speech,
His heavenly host to be my guard.

Against the demon snares of sin,
The vice that gives temptation force,
The natural lusts that war within,
The hostile men that mar my course;
Or few or many, far or nigh,
In every place, and in all hours
Against their fierce hostility,
I bind to me these holy powers.

Against all Satan's spells and wiles,
Against false words of heresy,
Against the knowledge that defiles
Against the heart's idolatry,
Against the wizard's evil craft,
Against the death-wound and the burning
The choking wave and poisoned shaft,
Protect me, Christ, till thy returning.

Christ be with me, Christ within me,
Christ behind me, Christ before me,
Christ beside me, Christ to win me,
Christ to comfort and restore me,

the celtic heart

Christ beneath me, Christ above me,
Christ in quiet, Christ in danger,
Christ in hearts of all that love me,
Christ in mouth of friend and stranger.

I bind unto myself the name,
The strong name of the Trinity;
By invocation of the same.
The Three in One, and One in Three,
Of whom all nature hath creation;
Eternal Father, Spirit, Word:
Praise to the Lord of my salvation,
Salvation is of Christ the Lord.

('St Patrick's Breastplate')

* * *

Jesu, Lord of heaven and the world,
　　To thee I make my prayer.
Jesu, Lord, I beseech thee
　　Against devils' temptations.
Jesu Christ, keep me always
　　Loyally to serve thee in my days.
Jesu, my body and my spirit,
　　All my strength and my thoughts
　　I give to worship thee,

ST PATRICK

And I pray thee, humble and meek,
That I never be on earth
    Turned to the lust of this world.

Mary, queen of heaven,
    Who fed Christ with thy milk,
Mary, upraise thy hand
    To the child of knowledge.
    Mary sweet, pray with me
That never may the caitiff Devil have
    Power over me,
Nor the world, my other enemy
And my flesh which is an evil enemy.

With watching and with penance.
    I would like
    To please Christ
In youth and in old age.

(*Beunans Meriasek*, 142–67)

12

ST NINIAN

ST Ninian was born on the northern shores of the Solway Firth around AD 360. His father was a converted chieftain of the Cumbrian Britons who wanted his son to be a soldier. Ninian, however, had other ideas and from a very early age was determined to dedicate his life to God. The great Celtic centres of learning were not yet established and, determined to receive a Christian education, the young Ninian travelled to Rome where he studied for many years. He was ordained priest and finally, in AD 394, he was consecrated bishop by Pope Siricus in order to return home to convert his native Scotland.

On his journey home he visited St Martin at Tours and was greatly impressed by this charismatic teacher. When he finally returned to the Solway Firth he built his first church at Whithorn, a small square building of local stone covered with white mortar, which became known as the Candida Casa, or White House. Ninian dedicated the church to his friend Martin of Tours, who died in AD 397, the year that it was completed.

From the Candida Casa, Ninian and his monks set out to convert the neighbouring Britons and the Picts of the former Roman province of Valentia. They were remarkably successful and Ninian, with his tall, soldierly build and his family connections, was able to talk on equal terms with the warlike tribal chieftains. The Candida Casa became a centre of Christian learning for many centuries after Ninian's death in AD 432.

Like his friend and hero St Martin, Ninian found himself a cave where he could retreat for days on end to meditate and pray. During the Middle Ages this cave became a focal point for many pilgrimages, and crosses have been carved in the cliff walls by the numerous devotees who made the journey.

Ninian's feast day is on 16 September.

Prayers of the morning

Thanks to Thee, God,
Who brought'st me from yesterday
To the beginning of today,
Everlasting joy
To earn for my soul
With good intent.
And for every gift of peace
Thou bestowest on me,
My thoughts, my words,
My deeds, my desires
I dedicate to Thee,
I supplicate Thee,
I beseech Thee,
To keep me from offence,
And to shield me tonight,
    For the sake of Thy wounds
    With Thine offering of grace.

(*Carmina Gadelica*, I, 99)

ST NINIAN

Be the eye of God between me and each eye,
Between me and each purpose God's purpose lie,
Be the hand of God between me and each hand,
Between me and each shield the shield of God stand,
God's desire between me and each desire be,
Be God's bridle between each bridle and me,
   And no man's mouth able to curse me I see.

Between me and each pain the pain of Christ show,
Between me and each love the love of Christ grow,
Between me and each dearness Christ's dearness stay,
Christ's kindness between me and each kindness aye,
Between me and each wish the wish of Christ found,
Between me and each will the will of Christ bound,
   And no venom can wound me, make me unsound.

Be the might of Christ between me and each might,
Be the right of Christ between me and each right,
Flow of the Spirit between me and each flow,
Between me and each lave the Spirit's lave go,
 Between me and each bathe the Spirit's bathe clean,
   And to touch me no evil thing can be seen.

(G.R.D. McLean, *Praying with Highland Christians*)

The Celtic Heart

So I am watching quietly every day,
Whenever the sun shines brightly, I rise and say,
'Surely it is the shining of His face,'…
Whenever a shadow falls across the window of my room
Where I am working my appointed task,
I lift my head, and watch the door, and ask
If He has come.

(Barbara McAndrew, from *Ezekiel and Other Poems*)

* * *

Father, praise Thee, now the night is over,
Active and watchful, stand we all before Thee;
Singing we offer praise and meditation:
                    Thus we adore Thee.

Monarch of all things, fit us for Thy mansions;
Banish our weakness, health and wholeness sending:
Bring us to heaven, where Thy saints united
                    Joy without ending.

All-holy Father, Son and equal Spirit,
Trinity blessed, send us Thy salvation;
Thine is the glory, gleaming and resounding
                    Through all creation.

(St Gregory, 6th century)

Still, still with Thee, when purple morning breaketh,
 When the bird waketh, and the shadows flee;
Fairer than morning, lovelier than daylight,
 Dawns the sweet consciousness, I am with Thee.

Alone with Thee, amid the mystic shadows,
 The solemn hush of nature newly born;
Alone with Thee in breathless adoration,
 In the calm dew and freshness of the morn.

As in the dawning, o'er the waveless ocean,
 The image of the morning star doth rest;
So in this stillness, Thou beholdest only
 Thine image in the waters of my breast.

Still, still with Thee! As to each newborn morning
 A fresh and solemn splendour still is given;
So does this blessed consciousness, awaking,
 Breathe each day nearness unto Thee and heaven.

When sinks the soul, subdued by toil to slumber,
 Its closing eye looks up to Thee in prayer;
Sweet the repose beneath Thy wings o'ershading,
 But sweeter still, to wake and find Thee there.

The Celtic Heart

So shall it be at last, in that bright morning,
    When the soul waketh, and life's shadows flee;
O in that hour, fairer than daylight dawning,
    Shall rise the glorious thought – I am with Thee!

(Harriet Beecher Stowe, Ireland, 19th century)

* * *

Praise God for the coming of morning,
Praise God for the start of the day,
For the tea in my pot
For the clothes that I've got,
And anything good for today.

Praise God for my car at the ready,
Praise God for the job that I've got,
For all that I'll learn
For the money I'll earn,
And the fact that I'm right there on top.

Praise God when my working week's over,
Praise God for the family at home,
For the things to be done,
For the weekend to come,
And the fact that I'm not on my own.

ST NINIAN

Praise God for all of the seasons,
Praise God for all that he gives,
For spring, summer and fall,
For the cold winter's call,
Because it gives us a reason to live.

Praise God for the strength of his shoulder,
Praise God when I turn 'Supa Nova',
For the way my life grew,
For all the people I knew
And the welcome God gives when it's over.

(Paul Randall-Morris, *A Word or Two*)

* * *

O God, who brought'st me from the rest of last night
Upon the joyous light of this day,
Be Thou bringing me from the new light of this day
Unto the guiding light of eternity.
   Oh! From the new light of this day
   Unto the guiding light of eternity.

(*Carmina Gadelica*, I, 33)

13

ST ILLTYD

ST Illtyd lived between AD 450 and 535. It is thought that he was born in Brittany and that he became a disciple of St Germanus of Auxerre at the monastery founded by Cassian at Marseilles. He is said to have come to England in about 470.

Other, non-historical, traditions claim that he was cousin to King Arthur and that he served him as a knight. It is said that he was converted to Christianity after an earthquake killed many of his companions on a hunting expedition.

Illtyd is known to have travelled around Brittany, Cornwall and Wales establishing monasteries and churches. It is, however, the monastery at Llantwit Major in the Vale of Glamorgan that is his most well-known foundation. Many young men came to study there and it became famous as a centre of learning. St Illtyd himself was a prodigious scholar, as the writer of St Samson's life tells us: 'Of all the Britons, he

[St Illtyd] was the most learned in all the scriptures, and in those of philosophy of every kind, specifically of geometry and of rhetoric, grammar and arithmetic, and all of the theories of philosophy.'

David, Samson, Gildas (the first British historian) and Paul Aurelian were all his students. According to legend, Illtyd enlisted their help to mark out a new boundary to the monastery lands. When the tide was out, Illtyd walked down the sands and marked a furrow with his staff along the low-water mark, then he and his students stood along the furrow and forbade the sea to pass. Needless to say, the sea obeyed! Illtyd was a conscientious and brilliant teacher, but sometimes he needed to withdraw and be quiet for a while. His favourite retreat was an oratory at Oxwith, but he is also known to have spent time at St Michael's Mount in Cornwall and in Brittany.

Illtyd's feast day is on 6 November.

Evening prayers

Let the flowers close and the stars appear
Let hearts be glad and minds be calm
And let God's people say Amen, Amen.

(Alison Newell, from the Creation Liturgy of the
Iona Community, 20th century)

The night was not made to be spent entirely in sleep. Why did Jesus pass so many nights amid the mountains, if not to instruct us by His example? It is during the night that all the plants respire, and it is then also that the soul of man is more penetrated with the dews falling from Heaven; and everything that has been scorched and burned during the day by the sun's fierce heat is refreshed and renewed during the night; and the tears we shed at night extinguish the fires of passion and quieten our guilty desires. Night heals the wounds of our soul and calms our griefs.

(John Chrysostom)

* * *

> May the Light of lights come
>   To my dark heart from Thy place;
> May the Spirit's wisdom come
>   To my heart's tablet from my Saviour.

> Be the peace of the Spirit mine this night,
> Be the peace of the Son mine this night,
> Be the peace of the Father mine this night,
> The peace of all peace be mine this night,
> Each morning and evening of my life.

(*Carmina Gadelica*, III, 337)

ST ILLTYÐ

I lie down this night with God,
    And God will lie down with me;
I lie down this night with Christ,
    And Christ will lie down with me;
I lie down this night with the Spirit,
    And the Spirit will lie down with me;
God and Christ and the Spirit
    Be lying down with me.

(*Carmina Gadelica*, III, 333)

* * *

The dwelling, O God, by thee be blest,
And each one who here this night doth rest;
My dear ones, O God, bless thou and keep
In every place where they are asleep;

In the evening that doth fall tonight,
And in every single evening-light;
In the daylight that doth make today,
And in every single daylight-ray.

(G.R.D. McLean, *Praying with Highland Christians*)

The Celtic Heart

God, give thy blest angels charge to surround
   Watching over this steading tonight,
A sacred, strong, steadfast band be they found
   To keep this soul-shrine from mischief-spite.

Safeguard thou, O God, this household tonight,
   Themselves, their means of life, their repute,
Free them from danger, from death, mischief-spite,
   From jealousy's and from hatred's fruit.

O grant thou to us, O God of our peace,
   Whate'er be our loss a thankful heart,
To obey thy laws here below nor cease,
   To enjoy thee when yon we depart.

(G.R.D. McLean, *Praying with Highland Christians*)

* * *

He lay with quiet heart in the stern asleep:
Waking, commanded both the winds and sea.
Christ, though this weary body slumber deep,
Grant that my heart may keep its watch with thee.
O Lamb of God that carried all our sin
Guard thou my sleep against the enemy.

(Alcuin of York)

sᴛ ɪʟʟᴛʏð

Bless to me, O God, the moon above my head,
Bless to me, O God, the earth on which I tread,
Bless to me, O God, my wife and children all,
Bless, O God, myself to whom their care doth fall;
    Bless to me my wife and children all,
Bless, O God, myself on whom their care doth fall.

Bless, O God, the thing on which mine eye doth rest,
Bless, O God, the thing to which my hope doth quest,
Bless, O God, my reason and what I desire,
Bless, thou God of life, O bless myself entire;
    Bless my reason and what I desire,
Bless, thou God of life, O bless myself entire.

Bless to me the partner of my love and bed,
Bless to me the handling of my hands outspread,
Bless to me, O God, my compass compassing,
Bless, O bless to me sleep-angel mine a-wing;
    Bless to me my compass compassing,
Bless, O bless to me sleep-angel mine a-wing.

(G.R.D. McLean, *Praying with Highland Christians*)

The Celtic Heart

In the stillness of the night

Come to me in prayer, said the Lord,

In the stillness of the night,

when the world sleeps.

Listen to me as I speak to you in the scriptures.

Receive me in the Eucharist.

See me in everyone you meet.

Love them, pray for all mankind.

Rejoice that you have found me, spend time apart to be with me.

Live in the world, but not of it.

You belong to me.

I have given you a precious gift, MYSELF.

Use it to lead others to me.

(Anne Ham, Cornwall, 20th century)

14

ST SAMSON

SAMSON was born in south-west Wales around AD 490. He was taken as a youth to be a student of the great teacher Illtyd at Llantwit Major and was ordained by Bishop Dubricius. He became abbot of a monastery on Caldy Island off the Pembrokeshire coast and from there he frequently visited Ireland. On one visit he purchased what the writer of his 'Life' calls a chariot, but which was probably a small donkey cart or wheelbarrow.

For a short period he withdrew to a hermitage on the banks of the Severn. When he returned to Llantwit Major he was elected bishop, but it was revealed to him that he should give up his monastic existence and become a *peregrinus*, or travelling holy man, leaving his native land to journey overseas.

Samson's method of travelling was unique. When he was travelling overland he was able to fold his coracle and sail and place them in his Irish 'chariot', and horses were hired to draw it along the road. On reaching the sea once more, the coracle was put back together and the chariot was lifted into it for the journey over the water. The chariot also carried all Samson's holy books, food and tools.

Travelling south from Wales, Samson crossed Cornwall from Padstow to Fowey, on what is now known as Saint's Way, and from there he set sail for Brittany. As he travelled, Samson claimed many people for Christ and took pride in scratching the sign of a cross on many a pagan standing stone.

In Brittany he founded a number of churches and monasteries, even travelling to Paris, where he was in contact with Childebert, King of Paris. His most famous monastery is at Dol.

Samson's feast day is on 28 July.

Travelling with Christ

> May the road rise to meet you
> May the wind be always at your back
> May the sun shine warm upon your face
> May the rains fall softly upon your fields
>   until we meet again
> May God hold you in the hollow of his hand.

(Old Gaelic Blessing)

ST SAMSON

Almighty Lord, thou God of might,
 Shield me this night and sustain,
Almighty Lord, thou God of might,
 This night and each eve again.

Sain me and save me from mischief whole,
 And from sin save me and sain,
Sain me my body and my soul,
 Each dark and each light again.

Bless me the land my hope doth prize,
 Bless me the thing faith shall see,
Bless me the thing my love descries,
 God of life, bless what I be.

Bless the journey whereon I go,
 And bless the ground under me,
Bless the matter I seek to know,
 Glory-King, bless what I be.

(G.R.D. McLean, *Praying with Highland Christians*)

The Celtic Heart

God be shielding thee by each dropping sheer,
God make every pass an opening appear,
God make to thee each road a highway clear,
   And may he take thee in the clasp
   Of his own two hands' grasp.

(G.R.D. McLean, *Praying with Highland Christians*)

* * *

   May the everlasting Father throw
     His shield to shade you
Every east and west that you may go,
     His shield to aid you.

(G.R.D. McLean, *Praying with Highland Christians*)

* * *

   The blessing of God, be it thine,
   The blessing of Christ, be it thine,
   The blessing of Spirit be thine,
   On thy children be it to shine,
   On thee and thy children to shine.

   The peace of God, may it be thine,
   The peace of Christ, may it be thine,
   The peace of the Spirit be thine,
   Thy whole span of life to refine,
   All thy days and life to refine.

ST SAMSON

Shield of God in the pass be thine,
Aid of Christ in the gorge be thine,
Spirit-water thou dost design,
Every going thou dost design,
A land or an ocean design.

The Father eternal's shield thine,
Upon his own lit altar-shrine;
The Father's shield always be thine,
Eternal from his altar-shrine
Lit up by gold taperflame-shine.

(G.R.D. McLean, *Praying with Highland Christians*)

* * *

Alone with none but
Thee, my God
I journey on my way;
What need I fear when
Thou art near,
O King of night and day?
More safe am I within
Thy hand
Than if a host did
Round me stand.

(Attributed to St Columba)

133

15

ST COLUMBA

ST Columba (the dove of God) was born in the December of AD 520 in Donegal, Ireland. He attended a number of monastic schools and was later ordained into the priesthood. Until the age of about 40 he travelled throughout Ireland setting up monastic centres of learning, including those at Kells and Derry.

In AD 561 Columba was accused of copying a prayer book belonging to St Finnian without permission. He was reluctant to give up the copy that had taken so long in writing and Finnian was so enraged that a battle ensued. As a result thousands of soldiers lost their lives and Columba was overwhelmed with remorse. He vowed to atone for his actions by winning as many souls for Christ as were lost in the battle.

Forced to leave his beloved Ireland, he and 12 companions set sail in a wicker-and-hide *currach* (coracle) and landed eventually on the tiny island of Iona. Here he set about establishing a monastery which became known throughout the Celtic lands for its discipline and piety. His monks followed a very basic rule, eating only when hungry and sleeping only when tired. They lived only to glorify God and shared equally in tilling the land as in studying and copying the Scriptures.

As the community grew, so did its influence, and Columba became the friend of many a king. The nobility sent their sons to Iona for education and the monks travelled widely, setting up more churches and monasteries. In AD 574 Aedan MacGabrain, the new King of Dal Riata Scots, travelled to Iona to be consecrated by Columba. This was the first time a British ruler had been officially blessed by the Church since the departure of the Romans.

A week before he died, Columba travelled around Iona blessing and encouraging everyone he met. As he rested by the roadside, his favourite horse placed its head on the old man's breast, and Columba took this as a sign that the beast sensed he was soon to die.

During those last days Columba dictated a prayer for his monks:

> See that you are at peace among yourselves,
> my children, and love one another.
> Take the example of the good men of ancient
> times and God will comfort and aid you,
> both in this world and in the world to come.
> Amen.

Columba died at the altar of his church, his face radiant with joy and his hand outstretched in blessing.

He is known in Gaelic as 'Columcille' to distinguish him from other St Columbas who followed him. *Cille* means a monastic church, and it is in honour of his founding the monastic rule that most influenced the north of Britain that he was given the name.

Columba's feast day is on 9 June.

Love of place

The hum of insects met my ear,
    The gorse in gold was dressed,
And underneath the hawthorn near
    The robin built its nest;
The lark his sweetest song did yield,
    Which fell in liquid showers:
O, nought was like the Under Field
    All white with daisy flowers.

ST COLUMBA

Nor will it fade from memory's eye,
From memory's treasured store,
Till darkness shadows earth and sky,
And life itself is o'er.
A bliss by hidden hands unsealed,
To cheer my latest hours,
Is that hill-sloping Under Field
All white with daisy flowers.

(John Harris, *My Autobiography*)

* * *

Flower of the moor, to Nature dear,
And sweet as thou art free,
I turn aside from crowded paths,
To muse in peace with thee.

Thou fillest with thy pleasant smell
The down in mosses dress'd;
The gentle breeze flows freshly by,
And fans thy yellow vest.

The housewife loves thee, treasuring up
Thy fragrant form with care,
Should sickness come, or wounds, or sprains;
For thou has virtues rare.

How oft, when hands and head were tired,
I've paced the common brown,
Or stretched me by your scented banks,
As the great sun went down;

And heard mysterious murmurs sound
Along the solemn sod,
The whispers of Omnipotence,
The silent speech of God!

Dear child of Autumn, sweetest when
The robin pipes his quill,
Along the early harvest sheaves
Delicious camomile!

(John Harris, *Walks with Wild Flowers*)

* * *

November

Clouds tempest-strided, heavy-sounding rain.
Wind, darkness, cold, make up thy dismal train.
Gloomy November! How the rivers rise
And echo through the hollows! Sadly flies
The last leaf through the forest whirling round,
Then hurled in anger on the sodden ground.
Sudden the change! The flowers are drowned with tears:
The pastoral field-paths, muddy, tempt no more;

ST COLUMBA

The plover on the open land appears,
And little redbreast ventures near the door;
The ploughman blows his fingers by his team,
The farmer's cart rolls rumbling down the moor.
Books now, and fire, where happy faces gleam,
And cheerful chat, when day's hard toil is o'er.

(John Harris, *Shakespeare's Shrine*)

* * *

June

Green fields and music. Life a cheerful bard
With song surrounded, gushing where she treads,
Come joyous June. The great trees bow their heads
Full-leafed. On cliff and common hard
Are the marks of Summer's fingers. Beauty-starred
Are all the walks of Nature; gentle eyes
Peer out from grassy windows, and the skies
Are bridged with feathery clouds where angels glide.
Turn we to earth? The bryony and rose
In the green land are clustering side by side;
And clover-scents, in showers, are wafted wide
By village stile, and where the fountain flows
A thousand lyres ring on the gladdened plain,
Burst from the woods, and murmur from the main.

(John Harris, *Shakespeare's Shrine*)

The Celtic Heart

Thine be the grace of love when in flower,
    Thine be the grace of humble floor,
Thine be the grace of a castled tower,
    Thine be the grace of palace door,
    Thine be the pride of homeland place
      And its grace.

The God of life to encompass thee,
Loving Christ encompass lovingly,
The Holy Ghost encompasser be
Cherishing, aid, enfolding to send
    To defend.

The Three about thy head to stand,
    And the Three be about thy breast,
The Three about thy body at hand
    For each day, for each night of rest,
    The Trinity compassing strong
      Thy life long.

(G.R.D. McLean, *Praying with Highland Christians*)

ST COLUMBA

The standing corn is green, the wild in flower,
    The vines are swelling, 'tis the sweet o' the year,
Bright-winged the birds, and heavens shrill with song,
    And laughing sea and earth and every star.

(Sedulius Scottus, 9th century)

* * *

Iona, Iona, Iona,
The seagulls crying,
Wheeling, flying
O'er the rain-washed bay;
Iona, Iona,
The soft breeze sighing,
The waves replying
On a clear, blue day, Iona.

Iona, Iona, Iona,
The wild winds whipping,
Comfort stripping
With the gale's chill sword;
Iona, Iona,
The waters glisten,
The wild winds listen
To the voice of our Lord, Iona.

(From *Columba, the Play with Music*, Julie Boobbyer
and Joanne Sciortino, 20th century)

141

The Celtic Heart

Columba's journey

Great is the speed of my coracle, its stern turned upon Derry.
Great is the grief in my heart, face set upon Alba.

My coracle sings on the waves, yet my eyes are filled with tears.
I know God blows me east, yet my heart still pulls me west.

My eyes shall never again feast on the beauty of Eire's shore.
My ears shall never again hear the cries of her tiny babes.

Though my body speeds to Alba, my mind is fixed on Eire:
upon Ulster, Munster and Meath, on her beauty from Lenny to Linn.

In Alba their hearts are hard, their tempers jealous and harsh;
their bodies plagued with disease, their clothes thin and scanty.

But in Eire their hearts are soft, their tempers gentle and wise;
their women fair and kind, their men stout and strong.

The orchards bend double with fruit, the bushes are blue with sloes;
the plains are lush with grass, the cattle healthy and fat.

Tuneful are the songs of the monks, and tuneful the chants
    of the birds;
courteous the words of young men, and wise the words of the old.

My heart is broken in two for love of my beautiful land.
If death should suddenly take me, the cause is grief for my home.

ST COLUMBA

If all Alba were mine, from its centre out to its coast,
I would gladly exchange it for a field in a valley of Durrow or Derry.

Carry westwards my blessing, to Eire carry my love.
Yet carry also my blessing east to the shores of Alba.

Columba in exile
It would be delightful, O Son of Mary, to plough the blue seas to Ireland,
to measure the height of their waves.

We would sail around Moyn-Olurg, and plunge down through Lough
  Foyle,
hearing the swans in sweet song.

Flocks of gulls would rejoice, screaming and screeching with joy,
as our boat arrived in port.

In Ireland I was a man of power; when I left I was filled with grief.
In exile my soul was heavy.

I was forced to cross the sea. If only I had never waged that
wretched battle at Cul Drenne.

O happy my younger self, happy in my cell at Durrow,
happy in my own dear land.

the celtic heart

I remember the sound of the wind, rustling through the elm-tree
   leaves –
its music delighting my ears.

I remember the blackbird crying, flapping its wings in the wind,
its song delighting my ears.

I remember the call of the cuckoo in the bright mornings of spring,
its call delighting my ears.

I remember the cattle lowing, I remember the great stags leaping,
I remember the rivers babbling.

In truth I loved that land, I loved its rain, its sun.
O, to die in my home!

Columba's rock
Delightful it is to stand on the peak of a rock, in the bosom of the isle,
gazing on the face of the sea.

I hear the heaving waves chanting a tune to God in heaven;
I see their glittering surf.

I see the golden beaches, the sands sparkling;
I hear the joyous shrieks of the swooping gulls.

I hear the waves breaking, crashing on rocks, like thunder in heaven.
I see the mighty whales.

ST COLUMBA

I watch the ebb and flow of the ocean tide; it holds my secret,
my mournful flight from Eire.

Contrition fills my heart as I hear the sea; it chants my sins,
sins too numerous to confess.

Let me bless almighty God, whose power extends over sea and land,
whose angels watch over all.

Let me study sacred books to calm my soul;
I pray for peace, kneeling at heaven's gates.

Let me do my daily work, gathering seaweed, catching fish,
giving food to the poor.

Let me say my daily prayers, sometimes chanting,
sometimes quiet, always thanking God.

Delightful it is to live on a peaceful isle, in a quiet cell,
serving the King of kings.

(St Columba)

16

ST AIDAN

WHEN Columba died in AD 597, St Augustine was arriving in Canterbury. From this moment Britain experienced two distinct Christian missionary movements: the Celtic Church from the north and west and the Roman Church from the south and east of the country.

King Edwin of Northumbria married Ethelburga from Kent, and Ethelburga took to Northumbria the Roman Bishop Paulinus. Before long King Edwin became a Christian, and many of his subjects followed their king to be baptized. In AD 631 Edwin was killed in battle and his armies defeated. The pagan kings Penda and Cadwalla attempted to stamp out the newly founded Christian religion, but in 633 Oswald, Edwin's nephew, returned to re-establish his uncle's kingdom. He attempted once again to convert the people of Northumbria to Christianity.

Like many young noblemen, Oswald had been educated at Iona

and so it was to Iona and the Celtic Church (rather than the Roman tradition adopted by his uncle) that King Oswald turned for help in finding a missionary for his people. The monk Corman was the first to be sent, but he returned with the report that the people of Northumbria were an 'obstinate, barbarous people'.

The monk Aidan, who was present when Corman reported to the Abbot, replied, 'Brother, it seems to me that you were too severe on your ignorant hearers. You should have followed the practice of the Apostles, and begun by giving them the milk of simpler teaching, and gradually nourished them with the word of God until they were capable of greater perfection and able to follow the loftier precepts of Christ' (from Bede's *A History of the English Church and People*). Recognizing the wisdom of Aidan's words, the community consecrated him as Bishop and in AD 635 Aidan left Iona with 12 companions and travelled to Northumbria.

Aidan established a monastery on Holy Island, or Lindisfarne as it is also known, off the Northumbrian coast. The island was cut off twice a day by the tide, but looked directly across to the mainland and Oswald's castle at Bamburgh. Aidan the monk and Oswald the king supported each other in their work and Oswald often accompanied Aidan on his missionary journeys. Lindisfarne became the cradle of Christianity in north-east England and a great centre of learning and prayer.

When Oswald died, Aidan continued to travel alone, always by foot and always stopping to speak to both rich and poor. He baptized and befriended countless people, and was loved by all. By the time he died in AD 651 the fire of Christianity was burning brightly in Northumbria.

Aidan's feast day is on 31 August.

The Church

Shepherd's eye

Look down O Lord from heaven
on thy flocks and lambs;
bless their bodies and their souls
and grant that they who have received
thy sign, O Christ, on their foreheads
may be thine own in the day of judgement;
through Jesus Christ our Lord. Amen.

(Egbert, Archbishop of York, 8th century)

* * *

A blessing on Bishops and Abbots and Priests
On deacons and people and all.
A blessing on those who've been washed in Christ's love
And who strive to answer His call.

A blessing, a blessing, a blessing on you
A blessing, a blessing on all.

(*Gormola Kernewek*)

* * *

You, who work by Christ's side
And share His great love.
You, who touch with His hands
And feel with His heart.
His blessing is yours
His joy till the end.
Take it
Hold it
You are his friend.

(*Gormola Kernewek*)

* * *

Bishops

Lord Jesus Christ, Thou did'st choose Thine apostles
that they might preside over us as teachers;
so also may it please Thee to teach doctrine
to our bishops in the place of Thine apostles,
and to bless and instruct them,
that they may preserve their lives unharmed and
undefiled for ever and ever. Amen.

(Egbert, Archbishop of York)

Here be the peace of those who do your will;
Here be the peace of brother serving other;
Here be the peace of holy ones obeying;
Here be the peace of praise by dark and day.

(St Aidan's Prayer for Holy Island, 7th century)

* * *

The fisherman's church
I stand on the shore and wait.
Bring to me your loved ones.
I will shelter them under the shadow of my wings
As a hen gathers her young to the warmth of her breast.
Do not fear
They will be at peace.

(*Gormola Kernewek*)

* * *

Treslothan Chapel
Peal on, ye gentle preachers. Day is done,
And eve steals down the vale in garments grey:
I ponder in her shadows. One sweet spot
Is ever with me, as your echoes float
Above the tree-tops, like the sweep of wings,
A little grave it is among the hills,
Beside a Gothic chapel, and I seem
To hear the tread of those who haste to prayer,

Through primrose lanes, although I'm far away,
Here I have long desired to sleep at last,
When life, with all its cares, is at an end,
Among the honest, pious villagers,
Just at the foot of my old granite mount;
That when the cottager, his day's work done,
Sits in the dusk with baby on his knee,
What time the first few tapers gild the pane,
He, listening to the river at his gate,
May think of him who carolled through his moors.

(John Harris, *A Story of Carn Brea*)

* * *

Minister of the Trees
The Minister of the Trees! A lonely dell
Deep with grey oaks, and 'mid their quiet shade
Grey with the moss of years, yon antique cell!
Sad are those walls: The cloister lowly lade
Where passing monks at solemn evening made
Their chanting orisons; and as the breeze
Came up the vale, by rock and trees delay'd,
They heard the awful voice of many seas
Blend with the passing hymn – thou Minister of the Trees.

(Rev. R.S. Hawker of Morwenstow)

ThE CElTIC hEART

Touch the stones
My handsome
They're steeped in all our prayers
Touch them with your softness
Feel the laughter and the tears.
Kneel in quiet
My Robin
Kneel and add your prayers
The church is full of memories
Granite soaked for years.
Kneel in quiet
My Robin
Kneel
For God is here!

(*Gormola Kernewek*)

* * *

Green lichen clinging to cut granite stones
Grey sunlight streaming through glass,
Dust dancing on polished oak pews,
Lingering dreams of the past.
Hush as you enter. Walk softly my dear
Kneel at the altar and pray
For this is a house where many have come
And where Christ has chosen to stay.

(*Gormola Kernewek*)

ST AIÐAN

The hermit's hut

I wish, ancient and eternal King, to live in a hidden hut in the wilderness.

A narrow blue stream beside it, and a clear pool for washing away my sins by the grace of the Holy Spirit.

A beautiful wood all around, where birds of every kind of voice grow up and find shelter.

Facing southwards to catch the sun, with fertile soil around it suitable for every kind of plant.

And virtuous young men to join me, humble and eager to serve God.

Twelve young men – three fours, four threes, two sixes, six pairs – willing to do every kind of work.

A lovely church, with a white linen cloth over the altar, a home for God from heaven.

A Bible surrounded by four candles, one for each of the gospels.

(Traditional Celtic, 9th century)

The celtic heart

Let the rumble of traffic diminish
and the song of the birds grow clear
and may the Son of God come striding towards you
walking on these stones.

(Caroline Moore, for St Aidan's Chapel, Bradford Cathedral)

* * *

Jesu, Lord of earth and heaven
    always be worshipped,
Jesu Christ, he who serves you loyally
    in this world will not have sorrow.

(*Beunans Meriasek*, 3888–3891)

17

ST PAUL AURELIAN

PAUL was born around AD 495 in south Wales. Descended from Roman nobility, his family name of Aurelian is remembered to this day. He was educated by Illtyd at Llantwit Major and his companions included David, Gildas and Samson. After he was ordained he lived as a hermit in Llandovery, spending many years in isolation in his 'desert place'. Gradually, however, his piety attracted admirers. As increasing numbers of disciples joined him, he founded a monastery at Llanddensant, on moorland below the Black Mountain.

Eventually Paul took 12 of his students and left his native Wales. They travelled to the court of King Mark in Cornwall and on from there to the home of Paul's sister Sitofolla, who lived near Newlyn in Mount's Bay. The level of the sea was lower then than it is now, and large tracts of forest stretched out on land that is now covered by sea. By the shores of Gwavas Lake in the middle of the forest, Paul helped his sister build a small chapel. Many years later, when the sea encroached, the chapel was abandoned and rebuilt on top of the nearby hill where the village and church of Paul can be found today.

Paul and his companions travelled on to Brittany, where Paul was given the island of Batz on which to build a monastery. It was not long, however, before the local people begged him to become their bishop. He was consecrated at Leon, the town which now bears the name of St Pol de Leon and where Paul's bell is a treasured relic. The life of St Pol de Leon was written in AD 884.

Paul's feast day is on 10 October.

Pentecost

Jesus said: 'I have cast fire upon the world, and see, I guard it until the world is afire.'

(The Gospel of St Thomas)

ST PAUL AURELIAN

We beseech Thee O God open the heavens
From there may thy gifts descend upon him
Put forth thine own hand from heaven and touch his head.
May he feel the touch of thine hand and receive the joy
   of thy Holy Spirit.
That he may remain blessed for evermore.

(St Ethelwold, 10th century)

* * *

This day the earth became Heaven for us. Not because the stars descended from the heavens to earth, but because the apostles ascended to Heaven by the grace of the Holy Spirit, which was now abundantly poured forth, and so the whole world was transformed into heaven; not because human nature was changed, but because there was a change in the direction of the will. For there was found a tax-gatherer, and he was transformed into an evangelist. There was found a persecutor, and he was changed into an apostle. There was found a robber, and he was led into Paradise. There was found a prostitute, and she was made the equal of virgins. There was found wise men, and they were taught the Gospels. Evil fled away, and gentleness took its place. Slavery was put away, and freedom came in its stead. And all debts were forgiven, and the grace of God was conferred. Therefore Heaven became earth; and from repeating this again and again I shall not cease.

(John Chrysostom, *Homily on Acts 2*)

The Celtic Heart

Kindle in our hearts, O God
the flame of that love which never ceases
that it may burn in us, giving light to others.
May we shine for ever in your temple,
set on fire with your eternal light,
even your Son Jesus Christ,
our Saviour and our Redeemer.

(St Columba)

* * *

O High King of Heaven, Great Father of love,
Breathe your breath round me
Down from above.

O High King of Heaven, with your Son here below,
Walk by my side through life's
Ebb and flow.

O High King of Heaven, Great Spirit of might,
Pierce thou my spirit and fill
me with light.

O High King of Heaven, look down from your throne,
Guard me and guide me
For I am your own.

(*Gormola Kernewek*)

ST PAUL AURELIAN

O King enthroned on high
Thou comforter divine
Blest Spirit of all truth, be nigh
And make us thine

Thou art the source of life,
Thou art our treasure-store;
Give us thy peace and end our strife
For evermore.

Descend, O heavenly Dove,
Abide with us alway;
And in the fullness of thy love
Cleanse us, we pray.

(Irish, 8th century)

18

ST PETROC

ST Petroc is said to have been the son of a Welsh chieftain, born in the sixth century AD. As a young man, he was first educated in a monastery in south Wales and then travelled with a group of friends to study in Ireland. He stayed in Ireland for 20 years and then, still in the company of his group of friends, he set sail for Cornwall, landing in the Camel Estuary. On the spot where he landed Petroc established a monastic centre which later became known as Petroc-stow or Padstow.

Like most of his Celtic holy men, Petroc held to a very strict rule and each day from cockcrow to dawn he would be found standing up to his neck in the cold sea reciting psalms. His dedication drew many to him and the little community flourished. Eventually, feeling confident that the monks could manage for a while without him, Petroc set out on the pilgrimage of a lifetime. He visited Rome and then Jerusalem, and finally went on to India. Legend tells us that one day, as he stood by the seashore, a huge silver bowl appeared. Taking off his cloak and staff and putting them on the beach, Petroc stepped into the bowl and was taken by the wind to a small island where he lived for seven years, surviving on a single fish a day. At the end of seven years the bowl reappeared and Petroc returned to the shore, finding his cloak and staff safely lying where he had put them, guarded by a large wolf.

Petroc returned to Cornwall and built himself a small chapel and hermitage further inland from Padstow at Little Petherick. In due course he travelled even further inland, to a stretch of moorland where he built himself a small beehive hut. Unable even there to escape the students who continued to want to be with him, Petroc established his last and greatest community at Bodmin.

Petroc died on a visit to Padstow and was buried there, but the monks of Padstow eventually moved to Bodmin and took his bones with them. The ancient casket that held his bones can now be seen in St Petroc's Church, Bodmin.

Petroc's feast day is on 4 June.

A hermit's life

Grant me, sweet Christ, the grace to find, Son of the Living God
A small hut in a lonesome spot
To make it my abode.

A little pool but very clear, to stand beside the place
Where every sin is washed away
By sanctifying grace.

A pleasant woodland all about, to shield it from the wind
And make a home for singing birds
Before it and behind.

A southern aspect for the heat, a stream along its foot
A smooth green lawn with rich topsoil
Propitious to all fruit.

My choice of those to live with me and pray to God as well;
Quiet friends of humble mind
Their number I shall tell.

A lovely church, a home for God, bedecked with linen fine,
Where o'er the whitened Gospel page
The Gospel candle shine.

ST PETROC

A little house where all may dwell, and body's care be sought,
Where none shows lust or arrogance,
None thinks an evil thought.

And all I ask for housekeeping
I get and pay no fees,
Leeks from the garden, poultry, game,
Salmon, fruit and bees.

My share of clothing and of food from the King of fairest face,
And I to sit at times alone
And pray in every place.

('A Hermit's Prayer', Abbot Manteith, 6th century)

* * *

The woodland thicket overtops me,
the blackbird sings me a lay, praise I will not conceal:
above my lined little booklet
the trilling of birds sings to me.

The clear cuckoo sings to me, lovely discourse,
in its grey cloak from the crest of the bushes;
truly – may the Lord protect me! –
well do I write under the forest wood.

(Welsh clerk's song, 8th/9th century)

I have a hut in a wood: only my Lord knows it; an ash tree closes it on one side, and a hazel like a great tree by a rath on the other.

The size of my hut, small, not too small, a homestead with familiar paths. From its gable a she-bird sings a sweet song in her thrush's cloak.

A tree of apples of great bounty like a mansion, stout: a pretty bush, thick as a fist, of small hazel nuts, branching and green.

Fair white birds come, herons, seagulls, the sea sings to them, no mournful music: brown grouse from the russet heather.

The sound of the wind against a branching wood, grey cloud, river-falls, the cry of the swan, delightful music!

Beautiful are the pines which make music for me unhindered: through Christ I am no worse off at any time than you.

Though you relish that which you enjoy exceeding all wealth, I am content with that which is given me by my gentle Christ.

With no moment of strife, no din of combat such as disturbs you, thankful to the Prince who gives every good to me in my hut.

(Early Irish lyric, 10th century)

* * *

ST PETROC

O Son of the living God, old eternal King, I desire a hidden hut in the wilderness that it may be my home.

A narrow little blue stream beside it and a clear pool for the washing away of sin through the grace of the Holy Ghost.

A lovely wood close about it on every side, to nurse birds with all sorts of voices and to hide them with its shelter.

Looking south for heat, and a stream through its land, and good fertile soil suitable for all plants.

A beautiful draped church, a home for God from Heaven, and bright lights above the clean white Gospels.

Enough of clothing and food from the King of fair fame, and to be sitting for a while and praying to God in every place.

(St Manchon, 10th century)

* * *

Abba Antony said, 'Just as fish die if they stay out of water, so monks who tarry outside their cells or in the company of worldly men move away from their desire for solitude. Fish can only live in the sea, and so we must hurry back to our cells in case by staying outside we forget to care for what is inside.'

(Antony of Egypt, *Wisdom of the Desert Fathers*, 74 p. 24, trans. Benedicta Ward SLG, 3rd century)

Let no man who has renounced the world think he has given up some great thing: the whole earth set against Heaven's infinite is scant and poor.

(*Life of St Antony of Egypt*, Athanasius)

* * *

Longings

I wish, O Son of the living God,
O Ancient, Eternal King,
For a little hut in the wilderness
That it may be my dwelling.
A grey lithe lark to be by its side
A clean pool to wash away my sins
Through the grace of the Holy Spirit.
A pleasant church with linen altar cloth,
A dwelling from God of Heaven;
The shining candles above the pure white Scriptures,
This is the husbandry I would take
I would choose and will not hide it.

(Attributed to Bishop Colman, 7th century)

19

ST LEVAN

ST Levan lived during the fifth century AD and appears to have been a member of a small, Cornish noble family. As it is known that both his father and grandfather were Christians, this would date his family roots back to the time of St Martin at least.

St Levan established his cell near a well beside a small stream which tumbles down the West Penwith cliffs. His brother St Just made his home further round the coast, and his sister Silwen also lived nearby. St Levan appears to have been very fond of fishing and once when his sister and two small children visited him, he cooked them two of the chad he had just caught. The children ate quickly and one of them choked on the bones. The child came to no harm, but for many centuries the St Levan fishermen called the chad 'chuck cheeld', or choke child. In the little church that was built in the saint's name there are two fish carved on a bench end. Outside the church on the south side there is a giant boulder which has been dramatically split in two. Legend has it that St Levan struck the boulder with his staff and caused it to crack. He then prophesied that if the crack ever widened to be large enough for a pack horse carrying panniers to ride between the stones, the end of the world would come.

In nearby St Just there is an ancient tombstone with a Latin inscription, and it is known that the relics of Levan's brother St Just were housed there up to the fifteenth century and possibly beyond. Of his sister Silwen there is no lasting memorial, but St Levan, or Selevan, is said to have been the father of St Cuby. St Cuby, in true Celtic tradition, travelled away from his beloved homeland of Cornwall and went north to Ireland and Wales. His most famous foundation was the monastery of Holyhead on Holy Island, Anglesey.

St Levan's feast day is on 17 October, St Just's feast day is on the nearest Sunday to All Saint's Day, and St Cuby's day is on 12 December.

Each day with Christ

Iridescent
Sunlight, dappling blue
Among tawny grasses, bending
In the fragrant breeze.

Joy is a butterfly
Try and catch it in your hands
And it is gone.
Let it dance!
It is a fleeting pleasure.
A gift to delight the soul.
Enjoy! Enjoy!

(*Gormola Kernewek*)

* * *

July

Heat and hay-making! Through the scented grass
The sharp scythe rustles, bringing music dear
With pastoral echoes to the listening ear;
While, in the sunshine, boy and buxom lass
Raise clover-ridges. As the gate we pass
Leading into the meadow, gales of glee
Come floating breeze-blown over lake and lea.
In the tree's shadow by the panting kine,

169

The Celtic Heart

Rambles the angler by the limpid stream:
The earth is full of charity Divine;
Waves the green corn where glancing swallows gleam.
The lanes are loveliness where fair things dream.
A mystery fills creation. Earth and sea,
And fen, and forest, whisper, Lord, of Thee.

(John Harris, *Shakespeare's Shrine*)

* * *

A Cornish thanksgiving
For silver fish to fill our nets
For corn to make our bread
For milk and cream to brim the churn.
For tin and clay and lead.
For sunshine, flower and fields of hay
For shimmering seas of blue
For laughing children 'neath our skies
Our thanks, O Lord, to you!

(*Gormola Kernewek*)

* * *

May every task be done with joy
And every word that we employ
Show the Lord in Heaven above
That all we do, we do for love.

(*Gormola Kernewek*)

ST Levan

Give us, O God, our morning bread,
The soul by body nourished;
Give us, O God, the perfect bread,
Sufficiently at evening fed.

Give us, O God, milk-honey yield,
The strength and cream of fragrant field;
God, give us rest, our eyelids sealed,
Thy Rock of covenant our shield.

Give us this night the living fare,
This night the saving drink be there;
This night, for heaven to prepare,
Give us the cup of Mary fair.

Be with us ever night and day,
In light and darkness, be our stay,
With us, abed or up, alway,
In talk, in walk, and when we pray.

(G.R.D. McLean, *Praying with Highland Christians*)

* * *

O God, all thanks be unto thee,
O God, all praise be unto thee,
O God, worship be unto thee,
For all that thou hast given me.

τϧε cελτιc ϧεαρτ

As thou didst give my body life
To earn for me my drink and food,
So grant to me eternal life
To show forth all thy glory good.

Through all my life grant to me grace,
Life grant me at the hour of death;
God with me at my leaving breath,
God with me in deep currents' race.

O God, in the breath's parting sigh,
O, with my soul in currents deep,
Sounding the ford within thy keep,
Crossing the deep floods, God be nigh.

(G.R.D. McLean, *Praying with Highland Christians*)

* * *

A joyous life I pray for thee,
Honour, estate and good repute,
No sigh from thy breast heaving be,
    From thine eye no tear of suit.

No hindrance on thy path to tread,
No shadow on thy face's shine,
Till in that mansion be thy bed,
    In the arms of Christ benign.

(G.R.D. McLean, *Praying with Highland Christians*)

ST LEVAN

O God of the heaving sea,
Give the wave fertility,
Weed for enriching the ground,
Our life-giving pouring sound.

(G.R.D. McLean, *Praying with Highland Christians*)

* * *

Be with me, O God, at breaking of bread,
And be with me, O God, when I have fed;
Naught come to my body my soul to pain,
Or naught able my contrite soul to stain.

(G.R.D. McLean, *Praying with Highland Christians*)

* * *

A mind prepared for red martyrdom.
A mind fortified and steadfast for white martyrdom.
Forgiveness from the heart for everyone.
Constant prayers for those who trouble you.
Fervour in singing.
Three labours in the day – prayers, work, and reading.

(From the *Rule of Columba*,
original now in the Burgundian Library, Brussels)

The Celtic Heart

I find I take great pleasure
When I hear the church-bells ring.
And the sound of choirs within them
As they practise hymns they're going to sing.
I take pleasure from the spider's web
As it hangs with silver dew,
And from the early morning skyline
As the sun breaks into view.

I take pleasure from the raindrops
As they fall softly on my face,
And royal swans upon the river
With their fine aquatic grace.
I find I get much pleasure from
The movements of the breeze
And the way a shadow dances
With the leaves upon the trees.

I take pleasure from the books I read,
And the songs I sometimes sing,
And get pleasure from good company
And the fellowship it brings.
And I derive much pleasure
Just from breathing good clean air,
And my solitary moments which I find
Are all too rare.

ST Levan

Then there's laughter from small children
As their little games they play,
The way they think, the things they do,
And the funny things they say.
I get pleasure from soft water
As it flows along the stream,
And how it emulates sweet music
As it bubbles fresh and clean.

But I find I get no pleasure
From the grasp and greed I see,
For I've found life's greatest pleasures
Are the ones we get for free.
They don't cost us any money,
They are around us all the time,
And if you look you'll find your pleasures
With the ease that I find mine.

(Paul Randall-Morris, *A Word or Two*)

the celtic heart

Today is a good day,
I thank the Lord;
Nothing to do but enjoy it,
I thank the Lord:
I sit 'neath an Apple tree
Which at this very moment in time
Has neither fruit nor flower,
Nor buds in their prime,
And I applaud the Lord.

It seems in His wisdom,
Whether right or wrong,
That I should find contentment
In the sweet bird-song,
And in blooms now appearing
On the walls and flower beds,
That still seem to struggle
To raise newly formed heads.

I look to the Heaven
And see carrion crow,
And a wild buzzard circling
While watching its foe.

ST LEVAN

I see chaffinch and bullfinch,
Both pecking with glee,
As they both hop with care
Round the old holly tree;

I've ducks in the garden
Who with consummate ease,
Seem to wander round flower beds
Just as they please;
Today is a good day,
I thank the Lord;
And I've really enjoyed it
So thank you Dear Lord.

(Paul Randall-Morris, *Poems from the Heart*)

20

ST BURYAN

St Buryan was born in Ireland, the daughter of an Irish king and said to be a friend of St Patrick. This would date her in the middle of the fifth century AD. She left Ireland in the company of other early saints and landed on the north coast of Cornwall near the present-day St Ives. Travelling inland, she made her home in the middle of the flat moorland of Penwith, at the spot which is called St Buryan to this day. Her name may well be derived from the Cornish expression *hi beriona*, which means 'the Irish lady'. The place where St Buryan built her little chapel developed into a small Celtic monastery and later on, in the tenth century, King Athelstan endowed a new church and established a college of canons in her honour.

Treasured in the Parish of St Buryan even today is this ancient hymn:

ST BURYAN

Long years ago across the Western water
Winds brought to this our shore
One glorious wilhen, a king's own daughter
To teach our land Christ's law.

The Saints of God His glory are
Cantate Domino, 'Alleluia!'

Throughout her days God's little flock she tended
A faithful shepherdess
Leading the sheep her patient love defended
Against the wilderness.

The Saints of God his glory are
Cantate Domino, 'Alleluia!'

Buryan's feast day is on the Sunday nearest to 13 May.

Love and marriage

Together we belong to be.
Holy three, be over we.

(A blessing for Cornish lovers, *Gormola Kernewek*)

* * *

Let us light a candle
For our love
To chase back the shadows
Of fear.

My light is for kindness,
Mine is for trust,
Together we'll draw
ever near.

Be with us O Father
Be with us O Son
Be with us O Spirit
Of Light.

Together our road
Will be gentle and wide,
Be with us and guard us
Aright.

(*Gormola Kernewek*)

ST BURYAN

A voice soft and musical I pray for thee,
And a tongue loving and mild:
Two things good for daughter and for son,
For husband and for wife.

The joy of God be in thy face,
Joy to all who see thee;
The circling of God be keeping thee,
Angels of God shielding thee.

(G.R.D. McLean, *Praying with Highland Christians*)

* * *

Thine be the grace of love when in flower,
Thine be the grace of humble floor,
Thine be the grace of a castled tower,
Thine be the grace of palace door,
Thine be the pride of homeland place
And its grace.

The God of life to encompass thee,
Loving Christ encompass lovingly,
The Holy Ghost encompasser be
Cherishing, aid, enfolding to send
To defend.

the celtic heart

The three be about thy head to stand,
And the three be about thy breast,
The Three about the body at hand
For each day, For each night of rest,
The Trinity compassing strong
Thy life long.

(G.R.D. McLean, *Praying with Highland Christians*)

* * *

Peace between neighbours,
Peace between kindred,
Peace between lovers,
  In love of the King of life.

Peace between person and person,
Peace between wife and husband,
Peace between woman and children,
The peace of Christ above all peace.

Bless, O Christ, my face,
  Let my face bless every thing;
Bless, O Christ, mine eye,
  Let mine eye bless all it sees.

(*Carmina Gadelica*, III, 267)

ST BURYAN

May God's blessing surround you
And love fill your hearts
May Christ walk beside you
And never depart
Holy Spirit keep you faithful
And strong to the end
As the stars light your pathway
Sweet blessings descend.

(*Gormola Kernewek*)

* * *

God's blessing be yours
And well may it befall you:
Christ's blessing be yours,
And well be you entreated;
Spirit's blessing be yours
And well spend you your lives,
Each day that you rise up,
Each night that you lie down.

(*Carmina Gadelica*, III, 211)

* * *

The love in your hearts
Is God's gift to you both.

The Celtic Heart

The joy in your hearts
He shares.
May his peace be to you
A light on your path
And a blessing to banish
All tears.

(*Gormola Kernewek*)

* * *

High King of Heaven look down from above
And give now your blessing on us and our love.
Sweet Jesus be with us and guide our feet right
For without you we'll falter by day or by night.
Great Spirit of power give us your fire
And lift our hearts heavenward, higher and higher.
O Trinity, mystery, bless now our love
High King of Heaven look down from above.

(*Gormola Kernewek*)

* * *

The Cornish child, the Cornish child
Whose birthplace was the moorland wild...
Has left her parents' roof today.
O, for her and her partner pray.

(John Harris, *My Autobiography*)

21

ST CUTHBERT

St Cuthbert was born around AD 636 in the Scottish border country near Melrose. While tending sheep in the hill country as a young teenager, he saw a vision of angels in the sky carrying a soul to heaven. Leaving the sheep, he went straight to the monastery at Melrose where they told him that the great St Aidan had just died. Cuthbert immediately offered himself for the religious life, vowing to continue Aidan's work in spreading the gospel throughout Northumbria.

When Cuthbert had been at Melrose for some years, he was sent with another monk to the monastery at Ripon. It was while he was serving as guest master at Ripon that he became aware of the bitter divisions between the Celtic and Roman Churches. The Abbot at Ripon was of the Roman persuasion and when he realized that Cuthbert's affiliation and sympathy were for the Celtic Church, he sent Cuthbert back to Melrose.

Cuthbert became Prior of Melrose and then, in AD 664, the year of the Synod at Whitby, he travelled to Lindisfarne (or Holy Island). His friend Eata became Abbot and Cuthbert was made Prior.

At the Synod of Whitby the decision had been made that the Celtic Church would come into line with the authoritarian disciplines of the Roman Church. Cuthbert was a peace-loving man who believed that it was quite possible for the two disciplines to live in harmony, and he conducted the life of the monks at Lindisfarne accordingly. The Roman tonsure and the Roman date of Easter were both adopted and Cuthbert improved the discipline of the monastery, but in all else, Lindisfarne remained distinctly Celtic in character.

His firm but gentle manner met with hostility from those who had been disappointed at the outcome of the Synod, however, and Cuthbert found the going hard. He decided to retire into isolation on an island in the Inner Farne, where he built a cell and oratory. Here he lived a hermit's life and in true Celtic tradition often stood waist-deep in the sea to recite psalms. Legend tells us that otters would come to warm his frozen legs.

After 10 years Cuthbert was persuaded to return to Lindisfarne as Bishop, but two years later he withdrew into solitude once more and died shortly afterwards. His body was buried on Lindisfarne, but later, in AD 995, it was taken to Durham Cathedral.

Cuthbert's feast day is on 20 March.

Home and family

God, bless the world and all that is therein.
God, bless my spouse and my children,
God, bless the eye that is in my head,
And bless, O God, the handling of my hand;
What time I rise in the morning early,
What time I lie down late in bed,

    Bless my rising in the morning early,
    And my lying down late in bed.

God, protect the house, and the household,
God, consecrate the children of the motherhood,
God, encompass the flocks and the young;
Be Thou after them and tending them,
What time the flocks ascend hill and wold,
What time I lie down to sleep,

    What time the flocks ascend hill and wold,
    What time I lie down in peace to sleep.

(*Carmina Gadelica*, I, 103)

ΤΗΕ CELTIC HEART

God bless the house from ground to stay,
From beam to wall and all the way,
From head to post, from ridge to clay,
From balk to roof-tree let it lay,
From found to top and every day
God bless both fore and aft, I pray,
Nor from the house God's blessing stray,
From top to toe the blessing go.

(G.R.D. McLean, *Praying with Highland Christians*)

* * *

Peace between neighbours,
Peace between kindred,
Peace between lovers,
   In love of the King of life.

Peace between person and person,
Peace between wife and husband,
Peace between woman and children,
The peace of Christ above all peace.

Bless, O Christ, my face,
   Let my face bless every thing;
Bless, O Christ, mine eye,
   Let mine eye bless all it sees.

(*Carmina Gadelica*, III, 267)

ST CUTHBERT

Bless, O our God, the fire here laid,
As thou didst bless the Virgin Maid;
O God, the hearth and peats be blest,
As thou didst bless thy day of rest.

Bless, O our God, the household folk
According as Lord Jesus spoke;
Bless, O our God, the family,
As offered it should be to thee.

Bless, O our God, the house entire,
Bless, O our God, the warmth and fire,
Bless, O our God, the hearth alway;
Be thou thyself our strength and stay.

Bless us, O God Life-Being, well
Blessing, O Christ of loving, tell,
Blessing, O Holy Spirit spell
With each and every one to dwell,
    With each and every one to dwell.

(G.R.D. McLean, *Praying with Highland Christians*)

22

ST HILDA

ST Hilda was born in AD 614, into the Saxon royal families of Northumberland and East Anglia. In AD 627, along with her great-uncle Edwin, King of Northumbria, Hilda heard St Paulinus preach. She was just 14 years of age and was so impressed that she was baptized by Paulinus that Easter in York. For nearly 20 years after that Hilda lived the life of a noblewoman at the royal palace at Yeavering.

When Aidan came to Northumbria to preach, Hilda decided to become a nun. She started out to join her sister Hereswid at the convent in Chelles near Paris, but she had not travelled far when a message came from Aidan asking her to return. Aidan took her on as a student and gave her a small plot of land by the River Wear where she could make a hermitage. In AD 649 he made her abbess of a religious house at Hartlepool, which she ran in accordance with the rule of the Celtic Church. In AD 659 she founded a monastery for both men and women at Whitby.

Whitby became a centre for learning where literature and the arts were encouraged and vocations fostered. The lay brother Caedmon, who stuttered badly, was encouraged to sing there, and the songs and stories he wrote helped those who could not read to understand the Scriptures.

Hilda and Cuthbert both worked tirelessly for a peaceful solution to the struggle between the Celtic and Roman Churches, and in AD 664 Hilda offered her monastery at Whitby as a meeting place for all the leaders. She hoped for reconciliation and perhaps compromise on both sides, and sided with St Colman in his arguments for the Celtic cause. But the brilliant Abbot Wilfred from Ripon spoke so eloquently on behalf of the Roman Church that the Synod decided that the Celtic Church must agree to come into line with Rome.

The Celtic delegates were bitterly disappointed. This, it seemed to them, was the end of the Celtic Church and the traditions they loved so much. Hilda, however, accepted defeat gracefully and loyally brought the monasteries under her control into line with Rome. Ten years later Hilda became unwell and remained ill for a further six years until she died in AD 680. On the night of her death, a nun at a monastery founded by Hilda in Hackness had a vision in which she saw Hilda's soul being borne up to heaven by a host of angels.

Hilda's feast day is on 17 November.

Baptism

In name of Father,
> Amen

In name of Son,
> Amen

In name of Spirit,
> Amen

Three to lave thee,
> Amen

Three to bathe thee,
> Amen

Three to save thee,
> Amen

Father and son and Spirit,
> Amen

Father and Son and Spirit,
> Amen

Father and Son and Spirit,
> Amen

(*Carmina Gadelica*, III, 11)

st hilda

A small drop of water
  To thy forehead, beloved,
Meet for Father, Son and Spirit,
  The Triune of power.

A small drop of water
  To encompass my beloved,
Meet for Father, Son and Spirit,
  The Triune of power.

A small drop of water
  To fill thee with each grace,
Meet for Father, Son and Spirit,
  The Triune of power.

(*Carmina Gadelica*, III, 21–3)

* * *

The little wave for thy form complete,
The little wave for thy voice so meet,
The little wave for thy speech so sweet.

The little wave for thy means requite,
The little wave for thy generous plight,
The little wave for thine appetite.

The celtic heart

The little wave for thy wealth at hand,
The little wave for thy life in land,
The little wave for thy health to stand.

Nine waves of grace to thee may there be,
Saving waves of the Healer to thee.

The fill of hand for thy form complete,
The fill of hand for thy voice so meet,
The fill of hand for thy speech so sweet.

The fill of hand for thy mouth so small,
The fill of hand for thy fingers all,
The fill of hand to make strong and tall.

The fill of hand for the Father one,
The fill of hand for God's only Son,
The fill of hand for the Spirit done.

Nine fills of hand for thy grace to be,
In name of the Three-One Trinity.

(G.R.D. McLean, *Praying with Highland Christians*)

ST HILDA

Sweet child
Warm, and moist with the dew of Creation
We offer you to the Father who made you
We offer you to the Son who died for you
We offer you to the Spirit.

My darling
We pour the water of new life upon
your dear head
May the Father give you strength.

My dear one
We pour the water of new life upon
your dear head
May the Son walk with you on your way.

My child
We pour the water of new life upon
your dear head.
May the Spirit fill you with love.

Fill you with love,
Fill you with love,
And bring you joy.

(*Gormola Kernewek*)

23

ST AILBE

ST Ailbe was born in Ireland during the fifth century AD. His mother was an unmarried slave-girl to Cronan, chief of the Eliach of Tipperary. When the baby was born Cronan ordered her to abandon it behind a rock in the open country and leave it to die. According to legend, the baby was discovered there by a wolf who suckled and kept it alive until its cries drew the attention of a passer-by. Having been taken into the village, the baby was adopted by a visiting Welsh couple, who called the baby Ailbe after the rock where he was found and returned with him to Wales.

As a boy Ailbe was always fascinated by nature, spending days alone in the countryside. He was especially interested in the stars and wondered who had made them. He questioned a visiting priest, who talked to him about God. The priest did his best to answer the boy's questions and Ailbe was baptized. As he grew, Ailbe continued to live in the wild, open countryside. Legend says that he was present when

Non gave birth to her stillborn child on the mountainside at Bryn y Garn, and that Ailbe revived the child by plunging it into ice-cold water. The child grew up to be David, the patron saint of Wales.

Ailbe returned to Ireland, where he became a monk and was later consecrated as bishop, founding a monastery at Munster. He died in AD 527.

Legend tells us that he retained his interest in wild creatures even though he rose to the rank of bishop. One day, it is recorded, he saved the life of a wolf being chased by hunters by hiding it under his cloak. He refused to give it up, saying softly to the wolf, 'Ah, my friend! When I was feeble and friendless, you protected me, and now I will do the same for you.'

For those who are sick

We open the roof
to lay our loved ones
at your feet.

Great King
Surround them with
the shining presence
of your love.

Loving Saviour
Heal their hurts
with your
tender touch.

Spirit of Fire
Give them
New life!

(*Gormola Kernewek*)

ST AILBE

See where he walks
With love in his face.
The sick
They touch his hem.
He looks so tired
And yet he loves.
Dear of Him.
He weeps for you
He weeps for me
Dear my Lord
He weeps.

(*Gormola Kernewek*)

Death

Those whom God loves die young;
They see no evil days;
No falsehood taints their tongue
No wickedness their ways.
Baptized, and so made sure
To win their safe abode
What could we pray for more?
They die, and are with God.

(Parson R.S. Hawker of Morwenstow, 19th century)

At the funeral of a child in this churchyard, the grave by a stunted tree, there broke in during the versicles an exquisite trill of song. It was last week. On looking up I saw a robin among the boughs not a yard from my head. We said the service together that Bird and I. At the close of every sentence came a still small sound like an infant's laugh, a cry of innocent gladness. From the Angel was it or the Bird? 'UBI AVES (IBI ANGELI)'

(Parson R.S. Hawker)

* * *

Remember, O friend, your end.

Now you are strong and fit, filled with ambition, boasting of your achievements; but all your success is a mere passing shadow.

Remember you are made of clay, and to clay you will return.

Now you are healthy and handsome, filled with energy, proud of your work; but all your joys are mere passing shadows.

Remember your life is the breath of God, which at death will depart.

Now your life on earth is solid and stable; but soon it will dissolve, your body crumbling to dust.

Remember, O friend, your end.

(Author unknown)

ST AILBE

There are things that you might read in the book of the Saltair na
    Rann
That are fully enough to beguile the reason out of a man,
The lawns of heaven, they say, are as wide as from here to the sun;
Twelve of them, silver-soiled, and kind to the feet that run.

All day you might travel that sward, nor be tired as we are here,
For Paradise air is of ether; lustrous it is and clear:
There's no wind to cast the blossoms in that place the sages call

The Heaven of the Wondrous Ether; – no wind, nor breezes at all.
But it's fresh, – the air – for the whole of it moves like the tide on the
    seas
Ample to nourish the flowering lands, the fruited trees.
Each lawn has its silver rampart, its gate as wide as a mile,
And a bird, red-gold, above each gate, singing the while.
I believe I could spend a life-time exploring the High King's land,
His songful habitation, measured by his great hand.
Had I but the one I love to go bounding at my side,
I'd not ask to enter the city, I'd stay on the lawns outside.

('The Lawns of Heaven', from *A Celtic Anthology*, Grace Rhys)

the celtic heart

Before he leaves on his fated journey
No one will be so wise that he need not
Reflect while time still remains
Whether his soul will win delight
Or darkness after his death-day.

(Bede's 'Death Song', 8th century)

* * *

Thou God of salvation great, outpour
On my soul thy graces from above
As up the sun of the heights doth soar
And on my body outpours its love.

Needs must that I die and go to rest,
Nor know I where or when it will be;
But if of thy graces unpossest
So I am lost everlastingly.

Death of anointing, repentance due,
Death of joy, death of peacefulness giv'n;
Death of grace, death of forgiveness true,
Death that endows life with Christ and heav'n.

(G.R.D. McLean, *Praying with Highland Christians*)

Time is like the ebbing tide on the beach. You cannot see it move by staring at it, but soon it has run away from sight.

(Traditional)

* * *

> O may the Father clasp you in his hand,
> His fragrant loving clasp bring you to land,
> Across the flooding torrent when you go
> And when the stream of death doth blackly flow.

(G.R.D. McLean, *Praying with Highland Christians*)

* * *

Soon you and I will die. We do not know the day or the hour of death; God alone has such knowledge. But we can be certain that many more years have elapsed since birth than will pass between now and death. You say that you have no fear of death. I fear death because I fear having to account for my evil deeds before God. You say that you fear the process of dying. I do not fear dying because I know that God will not force me to suffer pain beyond my capacity to endure it. Elderly people like ourselves frequently make attempts to amend their behaviour, hoping that God will forgive them past sins and judge them on present goodness. God will not be swayed by that kind of calculation. It is the heart, not the mind, that needs to change: we must learn to love God more fully. And love coming from the heart makes no calculation. If a person loves God with his whole heart, he will entrust himself to God's love, without seeking to sway God's

judgement by displays of good behaviour. If my heart could change in
such a way, my fear of death would disappear.

(Pelagius, *Letters of Pelagius*, trans. R. Van de Weyer)

* * *

Almighty God, Father, Son, and Holy Spirit,
to me the least of saints, to me allow that I may keep a door in
    Paradise.
That I may keep even the small door that is least used, the stiffest door.
If it be in your house, O God, that I can see the glory even afar,
and hear your voice, and know that I am with you, O God.

(St Columba)

* * *

I am going home with thee
    To thy home! To thy home!
I am going home with thee
    To thy home of winter.

I am going home with thee
    To thy home! To thy home!
I am going home with thee
    To thy home of autumn, of spring and of summer.

ST AILBE

I am going home with thee,
    Thou child of my love,
To thine eternal bed,
    To thy perpetual sleep.

I am going home with thee,
    Thou child of my love,
To the dear Son of Blessings,
    To the Father of grace.

(*Carmina Gadelica*, III, 379–81)

* * *

The golden rays of sun fall now upon
The spot where once it stood,
A hill now barren,
But looked upon once in a different light,
As just a green and lonely place,
Where tortured beyond all hope they hung,
The thief, the robber, and the like.

But what did He, so nobler man,
What act did He commit?
None, save by the act, He tied the knot,
Between all souls and God,
And tied it binding fast.

(Paul Randall-Morris, *Poems from the Heart*)

24

ST GUENOLE

It appears from most accounts that Guenole's family came from Cornwall and that they were caught up in the continual battles and skirmishes being played out by the local Celtic chieftains during the fifth century AD. The family packed all its belongings in a boat and moved in haste to Brittany. Guenole (his English name was Winwaloe) was born soon after they arrived and proved to be such an intelligent, questioning child that his father took him to St Budoc and asked if Guenole could become a student. St Budoc knew Cornwall well and was sympathetic to the family. He allowed Guenole to stay and took a personal interest in his upbringing. St Budoc's foundation was on the famous island of Lavre in Brittany and was built in the ruins of a fourth-century Roman villa. As a teacher St Budoc's reputation was unsurpassed, and his students travelled through western seaways, taking the gospel of Christ to Ireland, Cornwall and Wales.

ST GUENOLE

Guenole longed to go as a missionary to Ireland, but he was still young and Budoc held him back. Eventually he told Guenole to choose 12 disciples and to go and establish a monastery in Brittany. Disappointed that he was not being asked to travel the seas, Guenole nevertheless set off to find a suitable site. The Celtic saints have always loved islands and the small group were excited when they discovered the little island of Tibidy, which was cut off from the mainland at high tide but from which they could wade ashore when the tide went out. They set about building their cells and tilling the soil, but after two years they realized that the island was far too small to accommodate them. They abandoned it and crossed the estuary to build again on the sheltered northern shores.

The monastery that Guenole founded there was known as Landevennec. It flourished and, although Guenole himself never did reach Ireland, his students travelled to Cornwall in particular and possibly on to both Ireland and Wales. The routes they used as they travelled are dotted with churches dedicated to their founder and teacher. The most obvious route is the Landewednack, Gunwalloe, Towednack route across south-west Cornwall, from whence the travellers could continue to Ireland or Wales when the weather permitted.

The monastery at Landevennec became a Benedictine foundation during the ninth century and is still flourishing today as the religious heart of the Breton people.

Guenole's feast day is on 28 April.

Easter and resurrection

He who made heaven as He went
unto the tomb, great is my longing
after Him. Christ, hear my voice, I pray
also that Thou be with me at my end.

Lord Jesus grant me the grace
that I may be worthy to have leave
that with thee today, surely in some place,
I may have a view and sight of Thy face.

As Thou art Creator of Heaven and Earth,
and Redeemer to us always,
Christ my Saviour, listen if Thou carest,
as greatly I would like to speak with Thee.

(Mary Magdelene, 'Resurrexio Domini', *Cornish Ordinalia*)

* * *

The boy's blessings
Son of David, joy to Thee!
I beseech Thee to save us
and to bring us to the Kingdom of Heaven.
Blessed is He who cometh
in the name of God, praise Him!
King of Israel, mighty Lord!

ST GUENOLE

Joy to Thee, Son of David
Son of God art Thou and man as well.
Save all Thy faithful servants!
Because Thou art come
in the name of God, blessed
I believe Thou art indeed.

Blessed indeed Thou art!
Happy he who can be worthy,
surely, to worship Thee faithfully.
Without guile right truly I believe
that through Thee we shall be saved
O Son of God, joy to Thee!

Joy to Thee, Lord of the world
and heaven also!
Grant me peace to come to thy place
with thy angels.

Joy indeed to Him who is very God
and man likewise!
Through Thee we shall all be
in truth saved.

The Celtic Heart

Jesus of Grace who art Son and Father
Full of mercy,
We all pray, joy to Thee
Most certainly!

Sweet Jesus of Nazareth,
joy to Thee unhindered
and great honour indeed!
Thou art the Saviour of the world,
And that surely I believe
Have mercy upon me.

('Passio Domini', *Cornish Ordinalia*)

* * *

Show me the way of life
My Lord
For in thy presence there is
fullness of joy,
and pleasure for evermore.
Not for me the small, dark grave.
I would live in light
where the sweet scented winds of
heaven lift my soul
to your dear heart.

(*Gormola Kernewek*)

ST GUENOLE

Golden bloom
on withered
thorn.
Golden life,
sunlit
against a slate grey
sky.
Golden gorse,
Shout 'Victory!'
over the winter
of our death.

(*Gormola Kernewek*)

* * *

If God had not intended to raise us up again, if it was His desire that we should all be dissolved and blotted out in annihilation, He would not have wrought so many things for us. He would not have spread out the heavens above, or stretched out the earth beneath. He would not have fashioned this whole universe, if it were only for the short span of our lives. The heavens and the earth and the seas and the rivers are more enduring than we are; ravens and elephants live longer, and have a longer enjoyment of the present life, and they are more free from griefs and cares. What then? you ask. Has God made the slaves better than the masters? I beseech you, do not reason thus, O man; nor be ignorant of the riches God spread out before you. From the

211

beginning God desired to make thee immortal. Ah, but thou wert unwilling!

(John Chrysostom, *Homily xvii on I Corinthians*)

* * *

Shadows
And if tonight my soul may find her peace
in sleep, and sink in good oblivion,
and in the morning wake like a new-opened flower
then I have been dipped again in God, and new-created.

And if, as weeks go round, in the dark of the moon
my spirit darkens and goes out, and soft, strange gloom
pervades my movements and my thoughts and words
then I shall know that I am walking still
with God, we are close together now the moon's in shadow.

And if, as autumn deepens and darkens
I feel the pain of falling leaves, and stems that break in storms
and trouble and dissolution and distress
and then the softness of deep shadows folding, folding
around my soul and spirit, around my lips
so sweet, like a swoon, or more like the drowse of a low, sad song
singing darker than the nightingale, on, on to the solstice
and the silence of short days, the silence of the year, the shadow,

ST GUENOLE

with the dark earth, and drenched
with the deep oblivion of earth's lapse and renewal.
And if, in the changing phases of man's life
I fall in sickness and in misery
my wrists seem broken and my heart seems dead
and strength is gone, and my life
is only the leavings of a life:

and still, among it all, snatches of lovely oblivion, and snatches of
    renewal
of wintery flowers upon the withered stem, yet new, strange flowers
such as my life has not brought forth before, new blossoms of me

then I must know that still
I am in the hands of the unknown God,
he is breaking me down to his own oblivion
to send me forth on a new morning, a new man.

(D.H. Lawrence, 20th century)

* * *

Risen Christ we welcome you.
You are the flowering bough of creation.
From you cascades music like a million stars
Truth to cleanse a myriad souls.

(A Celtic Eucharist, The Community of Aidan and Hilda)

The Celtic Heart

If I should never see the moon again
Rising red gold across the harvest fields,
Or feel the stinging of soft April rain,
As the brown earth her hidden treasures yields.
If I should never taste the salt sea spray
As the ship beats her course against the breeze,
Or smell the dog rose and the new-mown hay,
Or moss and primrose beneath the trees.
If I should never hear the thrushes wake
Long before sunrise in the glimmering dawn,
Or watch the huge Atlantic rollers break
Against the rugged cliffs in baffling scorn.
If I have said goodbye to stream and wood,
To the wide ocean and the green clad hill,
I know that He who made this world so good
Has somewhere made a Heaven better still.
This bear I witness with my latest breath.
Knowing the love of God, I fear not death.

(Poem written after D-Day, 6 June 1944, by Major
Malcom Boyle of the Green Howards, who was killed in
action in Normandy on 16 June 1944, to his great friend,
Captain E.B. Cottingham MC, Gloucester Regiment)

ST GUENOLE

Last night Christ the Sun rose from the dark.
The mystic harvest of the fields of God
And now the little wandering tribes of bees
Are brawling in the scarlet flowers abroad.
The winds are soft with bird song all night long
Darkling the nightingale her descant told
And now inside church doors the happy folk
The Alleluia chant a hundredfold.
O Father of your folk, be yours by right
The Easter joy, the threshold of the light.

(Sedulius Scottus)

25

KING ARTHUR

WHEN the Romans left Britain in AD 410 there followed a period of confusion. The Saxons were invading and the Celtic kings and chieftains squabbled and fought each other for power. This was a dark time in the history of Britain. Bit by bit the disorganized Celtic Britons fell back as the Saxons advanced and took over the land. Out of this chaotic period has arisen the story of a man who single-handedly united the remaining Celtic tribes to make a stand which for nearly 50 years halted the Saxon advance. This man was called Arthur.

In some Irish stories Arthur was a Cornish king who held court at Killi Wig (possibly Tintagel). In others he was connected with Carmarthen in Wales, and still other stories give him origins in Brittany. Whoever he was, king or not, this charismatic figure is known everywhere as Arthur, and many legends have come down through history about him. Merlin, a wise man or Druid priest, was his mentor and in true Celtic fashion his sword Excalibur was his help-meet. In AD 500 Arthur allegedly made a stand on Mount Baden in Somerset with his beleaguered army and Celtic warriors rallied to his side from all over the west. As a result the Saxons experienced their first real defeat. Arthur's army chased them back across southern England and for a short period the country experienced Celtic rule once more, with Arthur and his knights bringing back a period of peace and chivalry.

According to the *Annales Cambriae*, a monastic record kept during the tenth century, Arthur carried the image of St Mary on his shield and the cross on his tunic. He was certainly revered by later genera-tions as a great Christian leader, but recently fiction writers have questioned the presence of Merlin in his life and have suggested that Arthur was a true adherent of the old Celtic religion. Whatever his beliefs, his character and his deeds make him an important figure in the Celtic scene.

Legend attributes 12 victorious battles to Arthur and his army, and according to the *Annales Cambriae* Arthur and Merlin perished at the battle of Camlann (said to have taken place at the mouth of the Cornish River Camel). But did they?

In the west of Britain a legend spread rapidly that Arthur did not die. It said that he survived and was carried across the sea to the magical island of Avalon where he still sleeps with his warriors. If Britain needs him he will return.

To the British people, Arthur stands for hope and for peace, and his legendary doings are held in great esteem. Since the Middle Ages he has been known as *Arturus, Rex Quondam, Rexque Futurus,* or 'Arthur, our once and future King'.

Christmas

My handsome,
My Robin,
My Joy.
Come
Mary's sweet boy!

(*Gormola Kernewek*)

* * *

Softly the night is sleeping
On Bethlehem's peaceful hill
Silent the shepherds watching
The gentle flocks are still.
But hark, the wondrous music
Falls from the opening sky
Valley and hill re-echo 'Glory to God on High.'

KING ARTHUR

Come with the gladsome shepherds
Quick hastening from the fold
Come with the Wise Men bringing
Incense and Myrrh and Gold
Come to Him poor and lowly,
Around His cradle throng
Come with your hearts of Sunshine,
And sing the Angel's song.

Wave ye the wreath unfading
The fir tree and the pine.
Green from the shows of winter
To deck the Holy Shrine
Bring ye the happy children
For this is Christmas morn
Jesus the sinless infant
Jesus the Lord is born.

('Padstow Carol', *c.* 18th century)

* * *

We have heard this very night the song of Angels, but maybe Angels can only sing and that it is for the feet of children to dance in welcome to their king.

(Bernard Walke, *Bethlehem: A Christmas Play*, 20th century)

The Celtic Heart

I will grow some flowers in my garden
So that in Springtime He may have a wreath
Celandines shall be in it and the largest daisies
Primroses perhaps, so when Good Friday comes
And He must wear the dreadful crown of thorns,
He will remember then this other wreath,
And it may comfort Him.

(Annie Walke, *Bethlehem: A Christmas Play*)

* * *

Song of the Shepherds
O sweet Jesus, my dear,
Good morning. Hail, my Lord;
I kiss your sweet hands and feet
For you are God.

Mary, my Mother, Hail,
Good morning, Lady fair
I bring a wreath of my best love
For you to wear.

Joseph, my Guardian, Hail
Good morning, Sir. I am sure
You take such care of all of us
And love the poor.

kING ARThUR

O Holy Family
Hail – you – and you – and you
I wish a merry Christmas. Give
Us peace, Jesus.

(Rev. W.H.C. Malton, *Bethlehem: A Christmas Play*)

* * *

Lo! The Eastern Sages rise
At the signal from the skies
Brighter than the brightest gem
'Tis the star of Bethlehem.

Baalam's mystic words appear
Full of light divinely clear
And the import wrapped in them
'Tis the star of Bethlehem.

Joyful let us quickly rise
Still the signals in the skies
David's rod of Jesse's stem,
'Tis the star of Bethlehem.

(Traditional Cornish,
St Agnes, Mithian, Perranzabuloe)

The Celtic Heart

Like the last prophet, dark December comes,
Uttering the doom of things. Hears my soul,
And profit by the teacher. List the roll
Of surging waters. Not an insect hums;
Carols no bird; cold gloom fills up the whole.
The trees, leaf-stript, lift up their arms in vain
To catch the struggling sunshine. On their steeds
The winds are mounted, prancing o'er the plain.
Then up the hills, then down the vales again.
Like a tired friend returning through the meads
He loved in childhood, after absence long.

To cheer us with the converse, even so
Comes blessed Christmas with its holy song
To gladden once again this world of woe.

(John Harris, *Shakespeare's Shrine*)

KING ARTHUR

What was the first branch of those branches three?
It was righteous Joseph and blessed was he.

> O the leaves they are green and the nuts they are brown
> They are hang'd up so high that they will not come down
> They will not, nor shall not, nor must not be so.
> O go your way, green leaves, O go your ways, go.

What was the second branch of those three?
It was the Virgin Mary and blessed was she.

> O the leaves they are green and the nuts they are brown
> They are hang'd up so high that they will not come down
> They will not, nor shall not, nor must not be so.
> O go your way, green leaves, O go your ways, go.

What was the third branch of those branches three?
It was our Lord and Saviour and blessed was he.

> O the leaves they are green and the nuts they are brown
> They are hang'd up so high that they will not come down
> They will not, nor shall not, nor must not be so.
> O go your way, green leaves, O go your ways, go.

(Traditional Cornish)

A star shone forth in the Heaven above all the stars, and its light was inexpressible and its strangeness caused amazement; and all the rest of the constellations with the sun and moon formed themselves into a chorus around the star; but the star itself far outshone them all. And men began to be troubled, wondering where this strange thing arose. From that time forward every sorcery and every magic spell was dissolved, and every bond of wickedness was destroyed; the ancient kingdom utterly pulled down; and God appeared in the likeness of a man for the renewal of eternal life. That which had been perfected in the counsels of God began to take effect, and now all things were in confusion, because He designed to abolish death.

(St Ignatius, *Ad Ephesians 19*)

26

st kea

St Kea is a romantic figure linked in legend to the story of Arthur. It is quite likely that he was Sir Kay, Arthur's steward.

St Kea was born in Wales at the end of the fifth century AD. Like all the Celtic saints he travelled about, settling for a while in Glastonbury where he made friends with the historian Gildas and built his own hermitage at Leigh, on the sloping hills surrounding the shallow lakes. Then he journeyed on through Devon and Cornwall and over to Brittany. In Brittany he is known as St Quary and he founded a monastery at Cleder.

Many of the Arthur stories portray Kay as an impetuous young man ready to argue and often saying the wrong thing at the wrong time. But it is as a peace-maker that St Kea is best remembered. With the days of his unruly youth behind him, Kea eventually became a responsible abbot. When the continual conflict between Arthur and his nephew Mordred threatened to disturb the newly found period of peace after the battle at Mount Baden, Kea returned from Brittany to try and bring about peace between the two enemies. He did not succeed, but stayed with Arthur as he struggled to hold the old Kingdom together. He apparently managed to persuade Guinevere to enter a nunnery, and later returned to his monastery in Brittany, where it is believed he died.

Kea's feast day is on 3 October.

Blessings

May the road rise to meet you
May the wind be always at your back
May the sun shine warm upon your face
The rain fall soft upon your fields
And until we meet again
May God hold you
In the hollow of his hand.

(Traditional Irish blessing)

* * *

The love and affection of the angels be to you,
The love and affection of the saints be to you,
The love and affection of heaven to you,
To guard you and to cherish you.

(*Carmina Gadelica*, III, 207)

* * *

God's blessing be thine,
And well may it spring,
The Blessing divine
In Thine every thing.

(G.R.D. McLean, *Praying with Highland Christians*)

The Celtic Heart

God's blessing be yours,
   And well may it befall you;
Christ's blessing be yours,
   And well be you entreated;
Spirit's blessing be yours,
   And well spend you your lives,
      Each day that you rise up,
         Each night that you lie down.

(*Carmina Gadelica*, III, 211)

* * *

Deep peace of the running wave to you
Deep peace of the flowing air to you
Deep peace of the quiet earth to you
Deep peace of the shining stars to you
Deep peace of the Son of peace to you.

(Traditional)

* * *

May the raindrops fall lightly on your brow
May the soft winds freshen your spirit
May the sunshine brighten your heart
May the burdens of the day rest lightly upon you
And may God enfold you in love.

(Old Irish prayer)

ST KEA

The might and the comfort of the Father
   Be with us always!
Jesu, the Son full of grace
   Succour us evening and morning!
The holy blessed Spirit
   His grace with us that we may have,
Mary, Mother and Virgin,
   To God's mercy pray for us.

(St Silvester, *Beunans Meriasek*, 2735)